The Madman's Window

& Other Tales of the Antrim Coast

Colin Urwin

ORKNEYOLOGY
PRESS

Dedicated to the memory of my mother, Agnes Urwin,

who was my first storyteller,

and to my wife Carol,

who has a faithful, listening heart.

Published by Orkneyology Press

Stromness, Orkney Islands

www.orkneyology.com

ISBNs:

978-1-915075-12-3 – hard cover
978-1-915075-13-0 – paperback
978-1-915075-14-7 – ebook

Book sales:

https://shop.orkneyology.com/collections/orkneyology-press-books

Contents

Acknowledgements

My heartfelt thanks go to the lovely Rhonda and Tom Muir of Orkneyology Press – for their encouragement, friendship and love, which is all so freely and sincerely given, and for welcoming me to their beautiful and fascinating island home. In the process they have fulfilled more than one of my long-held dreams. I will always be grateful and hope to be able to repay at least some of their kindness.

Many thanks also go to Katherine Soutar for her wonderful artwork and to Maura Johnston for allowing me to use her beautiful poem, The Storyteller. I am deeply indebted to both.

Foreword

Whilst growing up as a child in rural Glenarm, County Antrim, over fifty years ago, my generation and I were, without realising it at the time, witnessing the final throes of a transition from the old order to the new. We were moving from a time when the ancient folklore, musical and oral traditions of the Antrim Glens had all but given way to the modern world. The society we inhabit today bears very little resemblance to that old world – for better or for worse – and without becoming too sentimental and nostalgic about it, there is no question that important and valuable aspects of our cultural heritage have been eroded.

This wonderful book brings to life a time before the tyranny of modern technology, when storytellers and musicians were still an integral part of our rural communities. Stories, poetry and recitation had been embedded in our towns and villages as part of an evolving continuum for millennia. This aspect of people's lives anchored them to their locality and fired the collective imagination of old and young alike. They are the reason why myths and folkloric tales told around the hearth of every home from generation to generation were enjoyed and venerated so much. A fascination in these tales and oral traditions persists to this day, and even now, after so much change, the stories and verse in this book still resonate in exactly the same way.

I have known Colin Urwin for many years. I first knew him when he was demonstrating his remarkable skills as a falconer at Glenarm Castle some thirty years ago and now he has emerged as a professional folk singer, songwriter and storyteller. In this book he has created original stories built around fragments of folk and family lore using the motifs and conventions of an ancient story-telling tradition. I rather like the description of them by one observer as "folktales of the future", as it seems to encapsulate their timelessness. Crucially, these stories retain that vital element of mystery, suspense and haunting spirituality that captures the reader's imagination at the beginning and hooks them firmly in until the very end.

Randal McDonnell
15th Earl of Antrim
Chief of the Antrim McDonnells

Introduction

In the creation of these stories, I have drawn freely from the wells of historical events, family anecdote, personal experience and local folklore – rarely straying far from the Antrim coast in that regard. With each one I have attempted to merge these elements, to varying degrees, to craft something resembling an old folktale – perhaps more accurately a new folktale!

The ideas for some of these stories have been swirling around in my head since boyhood, mostly put there by my mother and other family elders. Later I was inspired by my future father-in-law, Tom O'Hara who I first met as a timid sixteen-year-old courting his daughter. Although I did not recognise it at the time, and nor did they, people like my mother and more especially my father-in-law were the last vestiges of the oral storytelling tradition.

During the ongoing lockdown of 2020, I had the time to develop some of the ideas I hoarded over forty years. I experienced an avalanche of creativity and wrote dozens of stories, songs and recitations – many of which are included here. Almost nightly I shared them with online audiences from around the world. My writing gathered momentum and other ideas rushed to my mind during daily walks to my favourite local beauty spot along the coast – The Madman's Window.

Yes, The Madman's Window is a real place, as are all the locations mentioned in the stories. To me folklore is most potent when it is rooted in the landscape. Indeed, it is by being so rooted that traditional stories and songs have the best chance of survival, otherwise they are at risk of being blown away on the wind and forgotten.

Many of the characters in these stories are also real, though they have been given different names to protect their identity. I have tried to honour the memory of many of the people I have loved and known or been told about by placing them in the stories. I hope my regard for these people, and for the often-harsh lives that they led, is apparent.

I hope too that my love for where I and my maternal ancestors come from shines through. The Antrim Coast is without doubt one of the most beautiful places in Ireland. The land, sea and skyscapes are sublime, and the wildlife is thankfully still relatively abundant and diverse. My great love for the natural world will also be obvious to the reader, but more than that I have tried to illustrate how our ancestors lived in greater harmony with their environment and had an inherent and better understanding of its rhythms.

It has been an absolute pleasure to write these stories: to go back over the lore and history contained in them; to revisit the beautiful settings and absorb their essence again; to breathe life into the characters who inhabit the paragraphs and pages; and to remember those who inspired me on this journey. Along the way there have been so many remarkable experiences and strange little coincidences.

At Nappin Cemetery, in a cool and overgrown nook near Garron Point, my wife and I were trying to locate the mass grave where the dead of the Enterprise of Lynn, wrecked at Ringfad, nearby, were said to have been buried almost two hundred years before. We were treading softly through the few weathered, tilted headstones and crypts when suddenly there was a tremendous crashing sound and a rush of wind, almost like an explosion. We ducked instinctively and one or two oaths slipped out.

It was a rockfall. Through the overhanging trees from the precipice above our heads a shower of limestone came tumbling down. It split the serenity of the late summer afternoon in that ancient burial place. We took it as a sign that we had outstayed our welcome.

On another occasion I was reading the final draft of "The Whuttrick, the Poacher and the Gamekeeper" to my wife Carol. I uttered the last word and then became aware that the expression on her face was one of astonishment. Slightly puzzled, I realised she was looking over my shoulder. I turned slowly to see a stoat *(a whuttrick)* peering at us through the window of my study. It was an enchanting moment of happenchance.

It is always a privilege to share these stories in schools and libraries, with community groups and at storytelling festivals the world over. I am continually struck by how some of them get under the skin of audiences and arouse genuine emotion. It pleases me greatly that they are often mistaken for traditional tales – which of course in many ways they are or, I hope, will become.

In 2020–2021 I recorded and produced a trilogy of albums combining some of the stories here with beautiful fiddle, harp and uilleann pipe music to create a rich and evocative soundscape. It is truly heart-warming to receive messages from people who have fallen in love with them. I am honoured when people ask if they might tell the stories themselves. I always say the same thing and I repeat it here...

"Of course! Stories are for sharing. Please feel free."

Colin Urwin
Glenarm
2024

The Storyteller

The magic of the storyteller
Lies
In the spark-flight and hand-sleight that flings
Words to settle soft as a selkie's skin.

The wonder of the storyteller
Lies
In the moons of nearly-known worlds
Where sorrow sings and souls' edges are blurred.

The allure of the storyteller
Lies
In the music of wild coloured charms
that weave through echoes new-born.

The power of the storyteller
Lies
In reflection and mirrors and spells
That whisper of us to ourselves.

Maura Johnston

The Seal's Skin

In the North Channel between Ireland and Scotland lie a pair of rocky islets four miles off the County Antrim coast. Known locally as The Maidens, they have been the site of a lighthouse since 1829. It used to be that two keepers were ferried out from Larne every month to relieve the home-coming crew. During bad weather, however, it was often too dangerous to attempt a landing. One month could easily drag into two.

In September 1834, a Scotsman then settled in County Donegal was sent to join a local keeper – an Antrim Glensman by the name of McAllister. Near the end of their stint, the weather blew up and they were stormed in for another two weeks. When the relief crew finally arrived, they were a little surprised to find neither the Scotsman nor McAllister on the small quay to welcome them. They landed their gear and still no one appeared. Together with the skipper of the ferry, they made their way up the steps with a strange sense of foreboding weighing on them.

When they reached the lighthouse, they found the door wide to the world. They went on into the mess room and the grisly sight that met their eyes haunted those men for the rest of their days. Slumped in a chair at the table was one of the keepers. He was barely recognizable as McAllister. His face was misshapen. His skin was black and purple. On his scalp was a deep gash and a cut was over his left eye. His nose had been broken. He was as dead as a stone.

The lighthouse and its curtilage were searched. In an outbuilding, a fresh seal pelt was discovered but nothing else out of the ordinary. Neither hide nor hair of the other keeper was found. Out around the island they went looking and eventually, huddled between two boulders, the Scotsman was discovered. His clothes were saturated and blood-stained, his boots full of seawater. He was barely alive. They half carried and half dragged him to the lighthouse and lit the stove. He was stripped of his wet garb and draped in blankets. His feet were placed in a basin of hot water. Not a drop of liquid nor a morsel of food could they get into him, and not a word of sense could they get out of him.

The deranged Scotsman, the gruesome corpse of McAllister and all their gear, including the seal pelt, were loaded into the boat and taken back to Larne. It was, to say the least, an unnerving trip for the lone ferryman. The Royal Irish Constabulary District Inspector was informed, and the Commissioners of Irish Lights dispatched a man from Dublin to investigate the strange incident. His name was O'Donahoe. He questioned the Scotsman in his hospital bed who was by now more talkative but making even less sense. After a long and difficult interview, the Scotsman asked for a priest. He died before he could finish his last confession.

Testimonies, such as they were, were taken from all the witnesses and O'Donahoe wrote a report for the Commissioners stating, "It appears the two keepers met in violent altercation resulting in McAllister's untimely death. The balance of the Scotsman's mind seems to have been disturbed, in all likelihood, by the consumption of poitín, there being a half empty jar found amongst his belongings. In view of the Scotsman's incoherent ramblings and fanciful claims, the exact circumstances of the incident cannot now be determined."

With both keepers dead, the coroner's inquest was brief. Next of kin were informed and the incident was discreetly written off. It would become the stuff of lighthouse legend and just another strange tale told in the mess or public house by the men who tended those lonely outposts of civilisation.

Some years later, O'Donahoe, now a retired man, was travelling in the Glens of Antrim. One evening he had occasion to take lodgings in a local hostelry. He found himself in a smoke-filled kitchen-room lit only by the flame of a peat fire and an oil lamp. Present were a few locals – fishermen mostly – and an old travelling woman taking shelter for the night in a nook by the chimney, which was not so uncommon in those days.

"Come in stranger. Sit yourself down and heat your feet by the fire. You'll take a wee colour of whiskey." O'Donahoe had a drink set before him. "What brings you to this part of the world?"

"Well," says he, "I am not altogether a stranger in these parts."

"Oh," said one, "have you kin hereabouts?"

And bit by bit, O'Donahoe's inquisitors pieced together his breed, seed and generation, making any connections they could, however tenuous. Before another round of drink had been called for, they had discovered the reason for O'Donahoe's previous visit. By the next they were discussing the strange occurrence of so many years earlier.

"And so, what did pass between you and this Scotchman?" he was asked. And whether it was the passage of time or the whiskey or the genial company that loosened O'Donahoe's tongue, he gave this account:

"Well, on his off watch the Scotsman drank some poitín. Feeling a little restless, he took a walk around the island just as the sun was slipping down behind the Antrim Hills. It was low tide and down by the water he saw what he thought was a young naked woman. He quietly approached her in the half light. When he came across a seal's pelt he seized it, believing he had surprised a selkie – a creature that is half seal and half human, if you want to believe such nonsense. Anyway, she pleaded with the Scotsman to return her pelt. He refused. He took her roughly by the arm and marched her up to the lighthouse. McAllister challenged him at the door.

'What in the name of God have you done man?'

'I have bagged us a selkie, and since we're stuck out here all alone, we might as well take advantage of our good fortune.'

'Are you mad altogether man?' cried McAllister. 'Unhand that poor girl.'

"But the Scotsman was wild with drink and lust, and defied his comrade. McAllister took off his big coat to put it over the girl's naked shoulders."

'Let her go I tell you or you'll bring a curse down on both of us.'

"The Scotsman tried to barge on past McAllister, which vexed him greatly. McAllister then struck the Scotsman a blow, and an almighty fight broke out. They were well matched, and for a long time traded blows and curses. At one point the Scotsman lifted a boat hook and made at McAllister, but just at that moment he felt a great thump in the middle of his back and the wind was knocked out of him. It was, he said, the young woman who had brought a large stone down on him right between his shoulder blades. In his rage, the Scotsman played swipe at the young woman and caught her face with the boat hook, taking her right eye clean out of its socket.

"The two men fought on to a standstill, neither able to get the better of the other. In the end McAllister staggered back into the kitchen and fell into the chair where, presumably, sometime during the night he died. The Scotsman gathered up the seal pelt and hid it in the outbuilding. He searched the island high up and low down for the young woman, but no trace of her could be found anywhere.

"Early the next morning the Scotsman awoke in a state of confusion and disarray, lying on his bunk. At first, he thought it must have been a terrible nightmare brought on by the poitín. When he saw McAllister and realised what he had done, he ran down to the water, intent on drowning himself. As he waded in, he was surrounded by two dozen or more great grey seals. They wailed and moaned, and the Scotsman was so terrified he withdrew and took refuge among the rocks where the relief crew found him later that day.

"More than that I cannot tell you," O'Donahoe said at length. "Except that it is my belief that the Scotsman was demented with the poitín. He and McAllister came to blows over God knows what. As for the existence of a selkie or a seal woman, well, quite honestly, I find that as far-fetched as tea from China."

Eventually the most aged of the fishermen said, "But what about the seal pelt Mr O'Donahoe? Where would it have come from?"

"It seems reasonable and likely to me that the Scotsman killed a seal or found one washed up dead and skinned it. A carcass was not found, but it had no bearing on the case anyway."

And then from her nook in the shadows the travelling woman who had been listening intently spoke up for the first time. "I beg to differ with you sir. I say the seal pelt has every bearing on the case."

A murmur went round the room and the retired Commissioners man felt his authority challenged. "Perhaps you would care to enlighten us Madame," said O'Donahoe dryly.

"Even after all these years if that pelt could be found, maybe the seal woman to whom it belonged would come forward."

This was too much for O'Donahoe.

"Nonsense woman," he cried, "utter nonsense."

"Find me that pelt and I will prove you wrong, sir," she said, and as she spoke these words, she leaned forward into the fire light. Her shawl drew back and revealed a hideous scar on her face and an empty eye socket. A gasp filled the air, and then there was silence. Even O'Donahoe was completely lost for words.

Whether or not the retired Commissioners man helped to locate the seal's skin after his encounter with the old travelling woman I cannot say. Let us hope that he did.

Swans

They say when swans are flying south
In long formations from the north
They navigate by stars,
And sing all through the darkest hours.

I'm told swans guide their youngsters from
A land of ice and midnight sun,
The old talk all in praise
Of ancestors and their ancient ways.

I've heard that swans mate for life;
The Cob and Pen in virgin white
Renew their vows each year
And always keep their loved ones near.

I saw swans dance once on a lake
And spread their graceful, feathered capes,
Heads bowed, necks entwined
And kiss since ages out of mind.

I know when swans give up the ghost
On silver, moonlit waters float –
Her shroud the clinging mists,
His restless soul forever drifts.

I lay beneath a starry sky
My wine–sleep full of mournful cries.
All though the night till dawn,
Wing tip to wing tip with a swan …

Marie and the Angels

The swans only ever came three or four times each year. No one ever saw them arrive. They just appeared in the bay overnight – a pen and a cob. In the morning they would drift in over the barmouth and up the river. That's when the people felt most ill at ease. Everyone knew then that someone in the village would not be long for this world. Who would it be? That was the question on the tip of everyone's tongue.

Sometimes it was a bolt from the blue. Like the time Singing Jimmy was walking about as fit as a fiddle one day, dropped like a stone the next. They said he must have had a weakness in his heart. More often it was somebody near death's door whose passing never came as such a shock. Like old Davy who'd been lying bad with apoplexy for months not able to speak or feed himself, or wee Jeanie with the shakes, God love her, she was very failed when the swans came to take her soul.

Marie was only five years old the first time she awoke to the idea that the swans had come to take away the soul of someone she loved. She saw them from the skylight in her attic bedroom, the only window in the house with a view out over the river. One of the swans raised itself up in the water and stretched out its long neck and raised its huge wings, before flapping them and settling back down again. That was when Marie got it into her head that the swans must be angels. She thought they were so lovely and white, and she wanted to show them to her big sister Nora.

She could hear her mother and father and the neighbours murmuring away downstairs. She didn't know what they were talking about, but she had sense enough to understand it was to do with Nora. She went downstairs and into the back room where Nora lay in a bed made up especially for her. The small room seemed crowded in the candlelight. She took her big sister's hand, which was lying limp by her side. It felt cold and damp. Nora's eyes opened wearily, but she smiled when they lit on Marie.

In her little voice, nervous and thin in front of the neighbours, Marie said, "Come up and see the angels, Nora. There's two of them."

"Take that wean into the scullery," someone said.

"She's alright," said her mother. "Just let her be." And then leaning into Marie she spoke in a gentler voice, "Whisht now pet, you'll scare your sister."

"She's not scaring me, Mammy," said Nora, and she squeezed her little sister's hand. "Tell me what the angels look like, Marie?"

"They're big and white with wings like a bird. What are they doing here, Nora?"

"Whisht now Marie," her mother said again, but Nora just smiled and put into words what everyone was thinking.

"They have come to take me away, darlin'."

"Away? Away where?"

"Up to heaven, love."

"But I don't want you to go up to heaven," said Marie.

"I know darlin'. But listen, I want you to do something for me. I want you to be a good girl when I'm away and remember me every night in your prayers. Will you promise me that?"

Marie nodded, but she would have promised her big sister anything. Nora closed her eyes again and let Marie's wee hand slip from hers.

Marie went back upstairs to watch the swans from her window. It was getting dark, but they seemed to glow as if they were floating lanterns, candlelit from within. Even when Marie closed her eyes tightly, she could still see them. Then she had an idea. She crept down the crooked stairs and slipped out the front door without anyone noticing. She gathered a few stones by the riverside and was about to start pegging them at the swans when she heard a voice.

"What harm did those birds ever do to you, little girl?"

It was an old tramp, a man of the roads, of which there were many in those days. "They're angels and they've come to take my big sister away to heaven," said Marie.

"I see," said the tramp. "And does your mammy know where you are and what you're doing?"

Marie dropped her head, and the stones. She told the tramp how she had sneaked out, and glanced towards her own front door. The tramp took her by the hand and led her back home.

"Let's not tell your mammy about the stones, eh?"

Marie's mother asked him in for a drop of tea and a bite of supper.

"Thanks Missus, but you've enough on your plate the night."

She insisted, for the tramp was well known to her. Everyone called him Oul Peter. He came twice a year at the same times and Marie's mother always gave what she could to him, and all the other poor men of the road who called at her door.

At the table by the window, Oul Peter was set down to a slice of buttered bread and a steaming mug.

"Ah, that's a quare good bowl of tae," he said as he slurped and ate. "The wee one tells me the angels have come to take her big sister away up to heaven."

"Aye, our poor Nora," said Marie's mother, her voice cracking with emotion. "The consumption has stolen the life out of her, and her only sixteen years old."

From the side of his eye, Oul Peter caught Marie studying him from the foot of the stairs. With a nod and wink in her direction he said, "She misses nothing, that wee one."

"Oh aye, she's been here before. Knows every word you're saying. God bless you, Peter, for bringing her back in."

Well, Oul Peter made his farewells, and Marie's mother pressed a few coppers into his hand.

"Thanks Missus," he said. "If there's ever anything I can do for you or yours …" And for some reason the little exchange of kindness made Marie's mother breakdown altogether, and tears streamed down her cheeks.

In the early hours of the next morning three sharp raps on the window of the small back room were heard. The old folk nodded and whispered that it was the Angel of Death, and young Nora's soul got away. The priest was there and led those assembled in prayer. The undertaker was sent for, and the bottom sash of the window was lifted to let the men pass Nora's coffin out into the street, to be bore away in the hearse drawn by a big, shining black horse.

At dawn Marie saw *three* swans. They paddled down the river together and lifted off into the breeze. She watched them till they were out of sight, and then she ran downstairs shouting, "Mammy, Mammy, the angels are taking Nora away up to heaven."

The family endured their loss like many of their neighbours had done before and many would do again. Six months later wee Marie began to cough up specks of blood and gasp for breath. The doctor confirmed it was tuberculosis – consumption of the lungs. There was nothing he could do. Her fate was in the lap of the gods. She was moved down into the small back room to a bed specially made up for her, and they waited.

When the swans appeared in the bay – a pen and a cob – and drifted in over the barmouth and up the river, everyone knew they had come for wee Marie's soul. The whole village was grief stricken. She was only five years old, and such an adorable child. The priest was sent for, and Marie was given the last rites. The women murmured the rosary in unison, and everyone waited.

Suddenly, Marie opened her eyes and stared into space. "Can you see the angels, Mammy?" she cried out.

The most fervent among them thought her spirit was at the gates of heaven.

"Do you mean the big white birds, darling?" her mother said.

"Yes, Mammy, are they there?"

Well, there wasn't a dry eye in that house or a heart that wasn't breaking. Marie was so anxious to know if the angels were there that her mother went upstairs to look out the attic window. She watched as three white swans paddled down the river and lifted off into the breeze, and eventually disappeared from her sight. With her heart aching, and blinded by tears, she came back downstairs, dreading to see her young daughter lying dead. But Marie was sitting up in the bed, eyes wide open. Her mother couldn't believe it.

"Are they there, Mammy? Are they there?"

"No darlin', they're away."

Later that morning Oul Peter the tramp was found curled up under the bridge down by the riverside. He had died during the night, starved from the cold they said. No one had even seen him come into the village. He hadn't knocked on a single door.

Marie rallied. She slowly recovered her strength. The doctor shook his head in disbelief and said it was nothing short of a miracle. The people just said it was not her time. It was the old tramp's soul the swans had come for after all.

As the years went by the swans returned, time and time again. They took the souls of Marie's mother and her father and all their neighbours, one by one. Marie lived till she was ninety-five. When her time eventually came hardly anyone noticed that two swans – a pen and a cob – appeared in the bay and drifted in over the barmouth and up the river.

As Marie lay down to take her rest she remembered, young and all as she had been, that night the angels came to bear her sister's soul away up to heaven. And she recalled too the night Oul Peter made a pact with the angels and gave up his soul that she might live another ninety years.

Marie gave thanks and smiled to herself. As she closed her eyes, she could see three white swans paddling down the river and lifting off into the breeze.

The Hired Lad

Liam Kinney was not yet twelve years of age when his mother walked him into Larne town from their wee bit of a farm in the hungry hills above Glenarm. They had set out at three o'clock in the morning and it was near seven when they reached the Fairhill steps.

"Put your boots on now," his mother said, and when she had her own boots buttoned up, she spat on her hands and tried to tame Liam's wild yellow hair that grew like a whin bush.

"Straighten yourself up now and take that hump off your back." She pulled and hauled at the lapels of his jacket and patted the dust off his ragged trouser legs that barely reached the bottom of his shins. Lastly, she retied his bundle. "Put that under your arm and keep it there. That's how they'll know you're for hire," she said, and then she proceeded to parade her son around the fair nodding to prospective farmers as she went.

They barely got a kindly look. All the while Liam saw farmers stopping with other young lads and feeling their shoulders and arms. "Can you milk, boy? Can you yoke a horse? Can you plough?" There were young girls there too. The farmers didn't manhandle them in quite the same way and they asked different questions: "Can you cook? Can you bake? Can you churn?"

Late in the morning a young farmer stopped with Liam's mother. He was gaunt and unshaven and looked hungered.

"Is he for hire, Missus?"

"He is of course," she said.

"How much are you looking?"

"Two pound ten shillings."

"Away outa that. What age is he?"

"Fourteen years old," she lied, "and comes from good hard-working stock. He can plough and milk and sow and reap and any other class farm work you care to put in his road."

"I'll give you a pound."

"I'll not go a penny below two pound."

Well, the farmer went up and Liam's mother came down, and after a lot of haggling and arguing, they eventually settled on one pound fifteen shillings along with Liam's board and keep in exchange for six months work – May until November. Liam's mother and the farmer slapped hands and the bargain was sealed.

The farmer pulled a silver watch out of his waistcoat pocket and checked it against the Townhall clock. "It's a quarter by eleven," he said. "I'll meet you back here at four o'clock sharp."

Nudged into action by his mother, Liam gave the farmer his bundle, such as it was, as collateral against the deal. In return the farmer took a half crown from his purse and put it into Liam's hand.

"There's your earnest money. The name's Hugh McKay of Raloo," he said.

"His name is Liam Kinney," replied Liam's mother as she took charge of the half crown.

"Well, don't be late," said McKay, and he strode away into the heaving throng as if he had other important business to attend to.

There were noisy salesmen Liam's mother called Cant Men. There were card trick men, ballad singers, fiddlers and pipers all vying for the attention of the fairgoers in the hope of relieving them of a few coppers. Liam was wide-eyed with fright and wonderment for he had never been further than the end of his lane, except for mass on Sundays and the National School on weekdays. He had never seen the likes before.

Of all the strange things Liam saw that day, the strangest was a huge, muscular black man who called himself Raz Tula. His skin glinted in the May sunshine like polished ebony. He was dressed in a leopard's pelt and very little else. He danced around incanting rhymes in broken English in a voice that boomed like a beaten drum. A crowd had gathered and Raz told the open-mouthed spectators that he was a witch doctor from deepest, darkest Africa. He was selling embrocations and potions passed down to him, he said, from tribal elders for generations. He claimed they had the power to cure everything from consumption to the pox disease, and a lot more besides.

Raz Tulla's eye caught Liam's and he flashed a gleaming smile the like of which no one had ever bestowed upon the boy before. Liam could do nothing but smile back, though his face burned bright red. At that, Raz winked imperceptibly at Liam and reached a big strong arm through the crowd and pulled the lad in.

"Here boy," he said, "take it. The cure for all your ills." And he thrust a bottle into Liam's chest. Liam took it involuntarily and Raz grasped his free hand in a firm shake to clench the mock deal. In the next instant Raz produced a silver shilling from somewhere, Liam didn't know where, and he held the coin up to show the people.

"Money well spent," Raz said, and ushered Liam back into the crowd just before he was inundated with people wanting to purchase one of his curative remedies.

Liam's mother scolded her son harshly and demanded to know where he had got the shilling. So quickly had Raz Tulla's hands moved that he had deceived even the watchful eyes of Mrs Kinney. The rest of the afternoon passed without too many more incidents, though there were one or two fights between drunken revellers. And a horse bolted, knocking over a stall of trinkets that the mob swooped down upon like gulls.

Well before four o'clock Liam's mother was waiting near the Fairhill steps for her son's new employer. He arrived promptly enough but it was obvious he was a little the worse for drink. That was nothing out of the ordinary for a fair day. Liam and his mother said their farewells.

"Work hard son and don't forget to say your prayers," his mother instructed. Liam could not answer for he had a lump in his throat the size of a duck egg and the tears were blinding him.

The farmer handed Liam back his bundle saying, "The half crown will come out of your wages," and then he added for good measure as if it had just occurred to him, "or your hide."

McKay swayed off to where his cart and horse were waiting. He clambered up and snapped the reins without so much as a by your leave. Liam half walked and half ran for the first mile before he decided to jump up on the bed of the cart and take his heavy boots off. And what a relief that was.

The farmer stopped at every hole in the hedge and more than one Stand and Dram on the way home. It was getting dark when the iron-shod horse and cart rattled into the farmyard. By now McKay's head was hanging low but the sound of his mother's welcome stirred him from his drunken slumber.

"Where the hell's gates were you to this time, ye big lump ye?"

Her son never answered. The old woman tongued a bit more but all her rebukes fell on drunken, deaf ears.

She was a wiry old witch of a woman, hardened by years of farm work and heartache. It was some minutes before she noticed Liam and his bundle in the back of the cart.

"And who the hell's gates are you?" she snapped, but before Liam could answer she started up again. "Another mouth to feed and him drinking every penny we get. What am I to do at all? I'm heart scalded, that's what I am."

With that she rounded on Liam. "Get you that cart washed down and that horse and all put away or you'll feel the back of my hand."

Tired and all as Liam was, he set to and did as old Ma McKay bid him. Her son stumbled across the yard to the beat of his mother's scorn.

"Hugh McKay, I wish I had drowned you at birth. It would have been better for me if I had. Heart scalded that's what I am."

It took Liam an hour and more to complete his chore, by which time Ma McKay was back in the yard.

"Here, boy. Can you milk a cow?" Without waiting for an answer, she bawled at him, "Come here with me."

They went into the byre where two cows were stalled. She threw a metal bucket at Liam and gestured him to start milking the number two cow while she took to the first one. Instantly Liam could hear the rasping sound of milk jets hitting the pail in the stall next door, but try as he might, he could barely get a dribble from his cow. Truth was he had only ever milked a goat before. Within a minute or two there were cramps in his wee hands, and he felt tears welling up in his eyes.

In short order the old woman was finished, and she came to see how Liam had performed. There was little more than half a cup of milk in the bottom of his bucket.

"What the hell's gates have you been doing. Get out of my road, ye big lump ye." she cried, "or I'll stick your head up that cow's arse. Another useless lump. What am I going to do at all? I'm heart scalded, that's what I am." And on and on she went.

Well, that was young Liam's introduction to life as a hired labourer on the McKay's farm near that wee place called Raloo outside the town of Larne. Only he was so completely exhausted when he threw himself down on the hay in the barn loft, he might have cried himself to sleep. Many a night after, he did just that.

Three months and more of constant working morning to night, and Hugh McKay's idleness and drunken threats, and old Ma McKay's constant nagging and curses, and nothing to eat but potatoes and buttermilk, and Liam had had his fill. Although he felt cruelly abandoned by his mother, a knot of homesickness had twisted itself inside his belly, and now he was hardly fit to eat or sleep. He was foolish enough to tell his employer he wanted to go home. Hugh McKay threatened him with a sally rod and seized all his clothes, and his boots. Liam pleaded to have them returned, but to no avail.

One night as he lay shivering in his underclothes in the barn loft and nothing but a threadbare blanket and a few meal bags to cover him, he heard an unearthly cry from the farmhouse. He lay for a while in the darkness petrified with fear and the cry came once or twice more. Then he heard sobbing like a child. The next thing Liam heard his name being called through the sobs.

"Liam. Liam. Come here, son. I need you."

It was the voice of Hugh McKay. Liam crept down the ladder and across the farmyard in his bare feet. He pushed the door open and went into the kitchen. He looked down into the bottom room and there was Hugh McKay sitting on the floor by his mother's bed, his head in his hands. With his heart in his mouth Liam went down into the room and there was old Ma McKay lying on the bed like some demented old hag with her jaw hanging open and her eyes staring wide. Liam swallowed a scream in his throat.

"She's dead Liam," said Hugh, sobbing and moaning like a child. "What are we going to do at all?"

Of course, young Liam didn't know what they were going to do. He was only twelve years of age. All he could think to do was bless himself. "In the name of the Father …" Then Liam and Hugh just stared at the old woman for a while.

Eventually Hugh got up and said, "I'll have to go and get me sister. She'll know what to do. Stay here with me mother till I fetch her back."

Liam wanted to run out of the room and never look back, but something kept him standing there, entranced, as Hugh took a key that hung around the old woman's neck on a cord. He went into a drawer in the dresser and from there he took out a box. From the box he took two big silver half crowns, and with shaking hands placed the coins to keep his mother's eyelids shut.

"Don't leave her till I get back, Liam," he said. And at that Hugh McKay hitched up the horse and cart, and away he went out the lane.

Liam was left alone in the room with the old woman. He had never seen a corpse before, and he was shaking like a leaf. He watched to see if her breast would rise. What a strange and frightening sight she was with her jaw hanging open and the two silver coins covering her eyes. The silence was overpowering. It was so strange to see her lying there, and not a single word coming out of her open mouth. To break the spell, Liam tore his eyes away from her and knelt down to say the Lord's Prayer. "Our Father who art in heaven …" but the urge to lift his head to see if she was moving was irresistible. That was when he noticed that from under her mattress poked the sleeve of his jacket.

"You oul bitch," Liam said out loud. "You bloody oul bitch."

Emboldened by rage, Liam tried to pull his jacket from under the mattress, but it was caught in the bed springs. He swallowed hard and lifting the mattress rolled Ma McKay over enough to find the rest of his clothes. As he did so the corpse nearly rolled off the other side of the bed and the silver coins slipped away. When the body fell back, Ma McKay's mad, staring eyes seemed to fix on Liam. He let out a fearful cry and began praying again. "Our Father who art in heaven …"

Liam quickly dressed himself and tied up a bundle with what was left over. As he was going out the door he stopped in his tracks and thought for a moment. He went back inside and, avoiding the gaze of Ma McKay's cold staring eyes, he groped in the bed clothes until he found the two silver half crowns. Out through the kitchen he went, taking with him a loaf and a wedge of cheese. But again, he stopped, for there on the dresser was the box with the key still in it. Liam went over and lifted the lid. Inside was more money than he had ever seen in his life. Gold sovereigns and half sovereigns; dozens of them. In an instant Liam snatched them up and was away with the lot before he could think another thing about it.

Out the door and down the lane Liam ran as if he was running for his life. They would not have hung such a young boy, but they might have sent him to Van Diemen's Land. But this was of no concern to Liam. All he was thinking about was getting as far away from old Ma McKay and her mad staring eyes as fast as he could. He was sure he could feel her breath on his neck. Every heart-pounding, breathless step of the way he was waiting for her big bony hand to fall on his shoulder, but he dared not look back.

Liam ran for as far and long as he could, but eventually the stitch in his side and the searing pain his lungs forced him to a standstill. He fell to the ground completely exhausted. When he eventually stopped panting, he looked around for old Ma McKay. Only when he was sure she was not behind him did he look at his surroundings. He was in a freshly mown hayfield with a great stack in the middle and there he took refuge, with his back to the sweet-smelling hay. His eyes darted this way and that at every whisper of the wind and every rustle of a leaf, but eventually tiredness overtook him, and he drifted off to sleep.

It was then the strangest thing happened. As Liam lay sleeping, old Ma McKay suddenly came to him. Her long grey hair drifted out behind her in the breeze like a banshee, and she was wailing and moaning like one too. As she came close Liam tried to raise himself up, but it was as if a great force was pressing down on him. He was helpless to move even a finger. Her jaw was hanging open and her eyes stared right through him.

"I want my gold back you wee thief. Not a single night's peace will you or your children have till the debt has been paid."

Her breath was foul, and Liam could feel her fists pummelling his chest. And then she was gone as suddenly as she had appeared. Liam looked about the field in the first rosy light of dawn. It was empty but for a few rooks and a hare. He gathered up his bundle and ran for all he was worth. Through fields and meadows and along deserted country roads Liam travelled all day, looking over his shoulder every few steps of the way.

That night he lay down in a sheepfold and the same strange thing happened. Old Ma McKay came to him like a Banshee saying the same thing.

"I want my gold back you wee thief. Not a single night's peace will you or your children have till the debt is paid."

Liam could smell her foul breath and feel the pummelling on his chest, but he was powerless to fend her off. And then, just like before, she was gone as suddenly as she had appeared. Night after night it was the same thing. As soon as Liam closed his eyes, no matter how exhausted he was, old Ma McKay paid him a visit.

Liam fretted about his mother and home, but he had sense enough to know that was the first place the law would come looking for him. Whether by chance or by instinct he had run off in exactly the opposite direction and now, a few days later, he found himself nearing the city of Belfast. If Liam had been bewildered by the sights and sounds of the hiring fair in Larne, Belfast was like a different world to him. The crowds and the clamour were vexatious to his already strained nerves. Like a hunted animal he kept to the shadows and knew he had to get away from the place.

Down by the docks Liam stared up at the forest of masts and spars and the tangle of rigging, and an idea began to form in his head. Suddenly he heard a booming voice behind him.

"Oy, mate. You with the blonde 'air!"

Liam knew the shout was directed at him, and he froze to the spot. The next thing, he felt a huge hand on his shoulder. "I'm done for," he thought. He turned around, but instead of a big Belfast Peeler it was none other than Raz Tula. Gone was the leopard skin and the broken English. He was dressed in smart working men's clothes with a scarf at his neck and shining leather boots. His accent was even stranger than before, but it was the same man alright. That gleaming smile was unmistakable.

"You've grown since the last time I saw you. What you doin' 'ere mate?" Raz said.

Liam was struck dumb.

"Are you lost mate? Where's your mam?" Raz asked as he looked about, but still Liam never spoke. "Ah. You're a fugitive."

"A what?" said Liam.

"You know, a runaway. You runnin' away from 'ome mate?"

Liam bowed his head to disguise the fact that his face had gone scarlet.

"I see," said Raz. "Maybe I can 'elp you then."

Raz led Liam along the quayside and into a cellar that sold beer and spirits. Over a pot of the vilest liquid Liam had ever tasted Raz told his young companion that he was in fact a docker from a place called Liverpool in England.

"I'm norra witch doctor from deepest darkest Africa," he said. "I come over to Belfast a couple of times a year and travel round the fairs sellin' me cures."

Liam nodded.

"I'm sailing back to Liverpool tonight. You can come with me if you like?"

Liam didn't know where Liverpool was, but he thought that if he went far enough away from Ireland old Ma McKay would not follow.

He was wrong about that. Every night without fail she came saying, "I want my gold back you wee thief. Not a single night's peace will you or your children have till the debt has been paid."

Well, to cut a long story short, Raz took Liam Kinney to the great city of Liverpool, where they had many adventures together. Liam learned a lot about the ways of the world from his new companion and they became the best of friends. Close as they were, Liam never told Raz or anyone else about his terrifying nightly visits from old Ma McKay.

In time, Liam went to America but her ghost followed him across that great ocean. Nevertheless, he prospered for he was no stranger to hard work. He invested his money wisely, and years later he became a very wealthy man.

Eventually, Liam Kinney met and fell in love with a woman to whom he proposed, and they were married. She wanted to start a family, but still every night Liam was visited by old Ma McKay giving her dire warning.

"I want my gold back you wee thief. Not a single night's peace will you or your children have till the debt has been paid."

For their honeymoon, Liam asked his new wife to come to Ireland with him. They visited his homeplace, but of course his mother was long since dead and the old farm had a new tenant. He went to the McKay farm at Raloo near the town of Larne where he had been a hired lad all those years before. It had fallen into disrepair. The thatch sagged and the once bright, whitewashed walls were green, with the mortar crumbling. He enquired from the neighbours and discovered that soon after the death of old Ma McKay, Hugh had let the place go to wreck and ruin. He had died in penury, and the two of them now lay in the graveyard down the road.

That night under cover of darkness, Liam found the last resting place of his old employers. With his bare hands he scooped a deep hole in the earth, and in it he placed a bag of gold coins. "This is all the money that is owing you," he whispered, "with interest, of course."

When he had covered it over and replaced the sod, he recited the Lord's Prayer. "Our Father who art in heaven, hallowed be thy name …" At the end of it he said, "Rest in Peace."

When the deed was done Liam went back to his wife. "Let us go home now and start our family."

He never did tell her about his time as a hired lad on that wee farm at Raloo near the town of Larne, or about old Ma McKay and the dreadful crime he had committed against her. But from that night on Liam Kinney slept soundly in his bed, for the debt was paid and, as we all know, a clear conscience is a soft pillow.

The Foster Mother

I mind the day they all arrived in a trailer from the farm,
My father and my mother with one in every arm,
My brothers and my sisters were told to lift one each,
Mine was warm and wriggly, and his skin felt like a peach.

We put them in an outhouse all decked out with straw,
Granny said, "Boys, them's the best wee pigs I ever saw."
And because I was the youngest my da said, "You're first, Son."
And I got to hold the foster mother with a teat for everyone.

Nine wee piglets chugged and sucked as I held that big stone
   jar,
And the wee boar I had carried in was the greediest by far.
Well, everybody took their turn, new-fangled as they were,
But the novelty fast wore off and soon no one seemed to care.

And I was left all the chores, but I delighted in the task,
And if you don't believe me well, there's no one left to ask.
I fed them morning, noon and night and wide-eyed watched
   them grow,
And with barrows-full of pig dung to the midden I would go.

Me da sold them off as weaners to a neighbouring farming man,
And I was broken-hearted, as you might understand.

But he let me keep my favourite so to him I gave a name,
And minded of a boy at school, I just baptised him Liam.

Liam grew up a mighty beast, stronger than a horse,
And I used to take him walking among the rushes and the
    gorse.
He was cleverer than any fox, more faithful than a dog,
His manners far from perfect, but God knows I loved that hog.

But then the awful day came: "Come on, keep up your chin."
My da said, as he explained, "We have to do Liam in."
"Murder him in cold blood," says I, "assassinate my pet?"
I thought them words would make him think, but my father's
    mind was set.

They were coming in the morning to do the dreadful deed,
A hammer to the forehead, throat cut and heeled up to bleed.
Big kettles of scalding water to shave his bristles clean,
And then rob him of his heart and lungs, his liver and his spleen.

I couldn't watch those butchers; they were a pitiless lynch mob.
With knives and saws and cleavers they went about their cruel
    job.
They hacked Liam into pieces, his shoulders were salted down,
His hams hung in the chimney where the peat smoke turned
    them brown.

With his blood they made black pudding, they boiled his head
    and feet.
My da liked the trotters best, but my ma preferred the cheek.
Those men bent to their gory work, they never stopped all day.
As Liam's kidneys sizzled in the pan they waited for their pay.

I peeked in through the window as they pocketed the coins,

Thirty pieces of silver paid for poor Liam's tenderloins.
Then my da poured out the whiskey and pipes began to reek
And they ceilidhed till the wee hours when the birds began to
    speak.

They devoured every part of Liam, nothing went to waste,
And unlike the folk that ate him his whole ancestry could be
    traced.
His hide went to the tanners, his bones were crushed for meal,
"The only thing they couldn't use," my da said, "was the
    squeal."

So many nights I lay in bed and prayed for Liam's repose,
In paradise with Granda, and our wee sister Rose.
I told them how I scratched his back and served his favourite
    treats,
How much he loved that foster mother with the nine red
    rubber teats.

That winter long my family lived on bacon, pork and ham,
But I survived on soda bread and my mother's homemade jam.
And as sure as Liam's in heaven from that distant day to this
Pig flesh, roasted, boiled or fried, has never passed my lips.

Tale of Two Friends

Once there were two boys. They were well known in their hometown of Larne as the best of friends. They were born within an hour of one another. They went to school together. Whenever you saw one you saw the other. The people always said that one shadow would do the both of them. They couldn't have been closer, not if they had been twin brothers.

One was called William. His father was a merchant who had shares in ships that sailed the world carrying whiskey and linen and bringing back tea and sugar, tobacco and timber. The other was called Robert. His father was a shipwright with his own small boat yard.

Robert was the oldest by a head, as the people used to say. Of the two he was always the more adventurous. When they climbed trees for rooks' eggs in the spring, Robert would always scramble out onto the slenderest branches. When they went swimming in the summertime, he would be the one who swam out the furthest. But for all that there was never any competition between them.

Being from a port town and with both of their fathers' connections to ships and shipping, it was only natural the boys should have an interest in them too. They were often to be found down along the wharf talking to the sailors. They would go aboard the ships and sneak up the rigging. Robert was always first to reach the crow's nest and would climb up to the highest yard. They imagined themselves as great seafarers and had lofty adventures with pirates off the coast of Barbary. They battled gales off Cape Horn and dreamed about the handsome, half-naked natives of the South Pacific Islands that they had heard about. They promised each other that one day they would run away and sail the seven seas together.

As the boys approached their fourteenth birthdays, they began making their plans in earnest. They spoke to the first mate of a merchantman due to sail for America. They offered their services as cabin boys and displayed their prowess in the rigging and at knot tying. The skipper agreed to take them on and told them to pack a pillowcase with extra socks and a shirt or two, and to meet on the quayside at six the following morning. You can be sure neither boy slept a wink that night.

The next morning young William crept down the creaking stairs of his father's big house. As he put his hand on the latch of the front door he heard his father's stern voice.

"William. Come into my study I would like to speak to you."

"Yes, Father."

"Tell me William, have you given any thought to your future?"

"My future, sir?"

"Yes. What do you see ahead for yourself?"

"I would like to travel the world, Father."

"I see. Well let me tell you, William, I have seen much of the world. It is a dark and frightening place. There is nothing but war and disease and treachery at every turn. Have you any idea how your mother might feel while you are gallivanting around the world?"

William had not.

"Your mother would be broken-hearted at your loss. If you should choose the path of the wanderer, you will be all but dead to those who love you."

William looked up at the big, long-cased clock. It was very close to striking six.

"I have other plans for you, William," his father continued. "I have had indentures drawn up. All you have to do is sign them and give me your oath that you will abide by their articles. After an apprenticeship of seven years, by which time you will be twenty-one, I will hand over all my business interests to you. You will be a very wealthy young man, William. Anything you desire will be at your fingertips. It would make your mother and me very happy."

And as his father's clock struck the hour, William signed himself up to a life of commerce and civic duty.

Time passed – sixty years in fact – and William had long since become the richest man in the town. He had been elected to the office of mayor and had all kinds of honours bestowed upon him. He had everything a man could want, but always he looked to the sea with longing in his heart. He often wondered how much more exciting his life might have been if his father had not scuppered his plans so long ago.

One morning, as he was walking through the town in a particularly buoyant mood, he came upon a tramp dressed in tattered rags with his hand out.

"Alms for a poor blind man. Alms for a poor blind man."

William felt in his waist coat pocket, but he had no coppers or silver. All he had was a gold half sovereign coin. On a whim he dropped the coin into the tramp's palm. The beggar knew by the weight of it what it was.

"Thank you indeed, sir. May God's blessing be upon you."

William hesitated and peered into the man's face. It was brown as a nut and bore the lines and scars of a life that had seen many adventures. But his eyes were clouded grey with cataracts.

Sensing William's close scrutiny the tramp said, "I was not always in need of the kindness of strangers, sir. Not long ago I was first mate on a clipper out of Liverpool. A sailor, man and boy for fifty-five years before my sight was taken from me."

"On what line did you sail?" asked William.

"I've sailed on them all, sir. Before I was eighteen years of age I had been around the world twice and seen both ends. I was born in this town seventy-four years ago, and I have come back to my home port to die."

Well, there was more conversation between the two but eventually William said: "Tell me, my friend, it wouldn't happen to be your birthday today, would it?"

"It is sir, but how the devil would you know such a thing?"

"Robert, it is I. Your best friend, William."

The two men embraced, and big salty tears ran down from Robert's unseeing eyes. William took Robert home and ordered his old friend to be given a bath and a new set of fine clothes. They sat down to dine, and William was regaled with stories about pirates off the coast of Barbary, gales off Cape Horn and the handsome, half-naked natives of the South Pacific Islands. After dinner they smoked a pipe and drank some French brandy, and before long they were singing sea shanties together …

Look ahead, look astern, look to windward and to lee.
Blow high, blow low and so sailed we.
I see a wreck to windward and a lofty ship is she
A sailing down along the coast of High Barbary …

William apologised to his old friend and confessed the reason he had not kept to their arrangements all those years before. There was no hard feeling between them. There never had been. They carried on their friendship as if they had never been parted.

After a while William said, "Robert, I want you to stay with me here in this house forever."

"That is very generous of you, William," said Robert, "but I am already far too deep in your debt. Blind I may be, but I am not deaf. I can hear your servants talk and I still have some pride left. I do not want to be a burden to you or to them."

"I have thought about this," said William, "and fair exchange is no robbery, so here is what I propose. I am in need of good counsel on all matters pertaining to my ships. You will be paid the going rate and therefore will be a man of independent means. But you must face facts, Robert, you are blind, so let my eyes be yours and yours mine."

"My eyes – yours? My eyes are useless, William."

"Nonsense! They have beheld so many things that mine have longed to see all my life. Stay here and tell me all the wonders you have seen, and in return I will look out for you."

To cut a long story short, the deal was struck and thereafter they were to be found out walking along the Bank Heads, arm in arm, William listening and Robert telling stories about pirates off the coast of Barbary, gales off Cape Horn and the handsome, half-naked natives of the South Pacific Islands.

Robert lived happily under William's roof for another twenty years, and still it wasn't enough time for him to tell his friend everything he had seen and done in his fifty-five years at sea. The two old friends passed away in their ninety fifth year, within hours of one another; Robert first and then William.

On the day of their funeral the whole town came out. They were buried side by side on a hill overlooking the sea. On their headstone is inscribed: *Only the best of friends can see the world through each other's eyes.*

The Drunken Piper

About a mile north from the town of Larne an outcrop of black basalt tumbles down into the sea. Through it a short tunnel was cut in the 1830s that later became part of the Antrim Coast Road. This work gave birth to the much-loved landmark known as the Black Arch. On the seaward side is a footpath. Through a gap in the seawall, steps lead down to a vertical cavern. The waves constantly surge up through it, spouting foam and hissing spray, which subsides just as dramatically with a hollow, guttering, sucking sound. To stand and gaze into its frothy, restless, swirling depths is an eerie experience. Close up it feels like a giant sea monster is breathing heavily in your face.

It is known locally as the Devil's Churn, partly because the sound is vaguely reminiscent of an old staff churn once used to make butter, and also because of the ominous air that hangs about the place. An old legend says that one night a drunken piper fell – or threw himself – into it. He was never seen again, but it is said that occasionally, when the tide is just right, his ghost can still be heard playing a haunting lament.

Not many people know that the piper's name was Eamonn O'Lynn. He was a man of small stature, being little more than five foot tall and of very slight build. His size and temperament were badly matched, for he was prone to getting into arguments and fights in which he invariably came off the worse.

He could, however, play the Uilleann pipes like nobody's business. Eamonn travelled around the countryside from fair to fair carrying his pipes in a leather case under his arm. In those days every town and village had fairs several times a year and some of them held competitions of dance and music and song. There were medals and honours to be won, and a very good musician could earn a decent living.

Good a piper as Eamonn undoubtedly was, he suffered from what they called "barrel fever". He could never resist the temptation of the Demon Drink. He always promised himself, "I'll only have a jar, or maybe two at the most, at least until the competition is over." But sure, don't we all know that the road to Hell is paved with good intentions.

When he arrived in a place on the morning of a fair, some shrewd publican was sure to spy him and entice him into his premises. After a feed of duck eggs and a wedge of soda bread washed down with a jar of porter, Eamonn would get the pipes out. As long as a steady flow of porter and whiskey came his way he would not budge for the rest of the day. In turn he attracted other players. The music and craic drew in the punters who spent their money over the shrewd publican's bar. It's a well tried and tested arrangement still practiced to this day in the better establishments around the countryside.

When the time came for the competition Eamonn was usually too far gone to perform to his best in front of the judges. Rarely did he gain the medals and honours his musical ability deserved. This only served to make him even more ill-tempered and fed his deep feeling of being hard done-by. He was often heard to bemoan, "I should have won that medal the day. Thon boy that beat me couldn't beat eggs."

And so it went on at every fair and every festival for years and years. And then in the year 1904, Eamonn pitched up to the first big Feis na nGleanns held at Waterfoot in Glenariffe. There were pipers and fiddlers and harpers and dancers from every corner of the country and some even came over from Scotland. Eamonn was determined to make a name for himself. And he did. That was the time they christened him the Drunken Piper.

In a foul mood Eamonn packed up early that evening and took the road back to Larne. He had a walk of twenty-odd miles ahead of him, but it was a warm June night, and he could still see well enough in the half light. Every step of the way he grumbled to himself, "There's not one of them boys is half the piper I am. If I have to sell my soul to the Devil I'll show them all next year."

By the time Eamonn was coming near the Black Arch the drink was wearing off, and he was feeling very tired and hungry. He sat down on the rocks just by the road and filled his pipe with tobacco, hoping a smoke would take the edge of his hunger before he walked the last mile or two into Larne. And all the while he was grumbling away to himself.

"I swear, if I have to sell my soul to the Devil, I'll show them boys next year …"

Just then a figure appeared beside him in the gloom. It was that of a tall man draped in a long black cloak with a big broad-brimmed black hat pulled down over his face.

"And what price," said the man, "would you be putting on your soul?"

"Eh? What do you mean, mister?" said Eamonn.

"It's a simple question. How much is your soul worth?"

Well, Eamonn looked the man up and down. "Who the Devil are you?"

At that the man threw his head back and laughed.

"Wait a minute, are you Old Nick?" Eamonn asked.

"The very same. Would you like to strike a bargain with me for your soul?"

Eamonn thought for a moment and then, as bold as brass he said, "I'll tell you what friend. If you're half as good as they say you are, it would be no bother for you to make me the best piper at the Feis na nGleanns next year and for seven years in a row, drunk or sober mind, and for that I'd let you have my soul."

"I think you've got yourself a deal, Eamonn O'Lynn," said Old Nick, and he clicked his fingers. The tobacco in Eamonn's old briar flared up red hot and burned out in that instant.

"Remember, Eamonn. In seven years from this night, I will return to claim your soul." And then just like that Old Nick was gone, leaving nothing but the stench of burning sulphur hanging in the air.

Time passed and Eamonn's reputation spread from fair to fair like wildfire. Eventually the Feis na nGleanns came round again. No sooner had Eamonn landed in the village of Waterfoot when a publican hailed him. By the time the pipers were ready to compete, Eamonn was barely fit to walk. He had to be helped up onto the stage. When he began to play his selection of tunes, the judges' mouths fell open. When he toppled off his chair sideways onto the floor and kept playing, everyone's mouths fell open. The judges didn't want to award Eamonn the title, but there would have been a riot if they had tried to deny him.

Eamonn was carried back to the bar a hero. The more porter was poured into him, the more jigs and reels poured out of him. And so it continued. The Drunken Piper just got better and better. No one had ever seen or heard the likes before. Six years in a row he won the title of Best Uilleann Piper at the Feis na nGleanns.

The next Feis was fast approaching, and only now did Eamonn begin to give any thought to his deal with the Devil. For weeks it kept him awake at night worrying and fretting. Eventually, he decided to repent, and he went to the parish priest and confessed all.

Understandably, the priest was horrified by Eamonn's behaviour, but of course being a man of the cloth, he was sworn to combat the Devil and all his evil works. After some consideration the priest spoke.

"Much as it pains me to say it, the Devil will be true to his word. So the solution to your problem is really very simple, Eamonn. Do not go to the Feis na nGleanns. If you cannot stay away, do not enter the competition. You will not win and therefore your deal with the Devil will be rendered null and void."

Well, Eamonn came away from the priest with a spring in his step. His name would still go down in history as one of best pipers, if not *the* best piper, in Ireland, and Old Nick could go back to Hell in a hand cart.

Eamonn decided to attend the Feis, just to tell them, "I'm not entering your oul competition. I'm going to let some of the rest of ye have a chance."

And then he landed into the pub, and the porter and whiskey flew. He played his pipes liked fury. The bar was heaving with folk anxious to hear and get a glimpse of the famous Drunken Piper.

As the drink started to take its effect, a wee demon appeared on Eamonn's shoulder. He began to whisper into his ear, "C'mon man. The folk are saying you're feared to enter the competition. That you're feared some young fella will beat you. C'mon Eamonn. Are ye a man or a mouse?"

Eventually, Eamonn could take it no longer. He bounced up out of his seat and staggered to the place where they were about to award the title to another piper.

"Wait!" said Eamonn, and he clambered up onto the stage.

When he began to play a slow air, he made the judges weep. When he played them a slip jig they danced as if they were possessed. And as he played a hurricane of a reel he toppled sideways from his chair and rolled off the stage and never even dropped a note. For the seventh year in a row Eamonn O'Lynn was crowned, Champion Uillean Piper at the Fies na nGleanns.

Well, Eamonn packed up his pipes, made his farewells and headed for home. It was the same long journey back to Larne under a full moon on a beautiful June night. He traipsed along the road, never meeting another living soul. Eventually the silhouette of the Black Arch came into view. In former days it had been a welcome sight, but this night Eamonn's heart was full of dread and sorrow. He sat down on the rocks and filled his briar with tobacco, and then the familiar dark figure of Old Nick appeared beside him.

"Well, well, well, Eamonn," he said. "You almost outwitted me, but not quite."

"Have I time for a smoke and one more tune?" asked Eamonn.

"Of course," said Old Nick. "But mind, we haven't got all night."

When Eamonn did not turn up the next morning a search was made for him. The old leather carrying case and his half-smoked pipe were found on the rocks near the Black Arch. Constables at the scene reported a curious stench of rotten eggs all around the place, and one of them found a strange scorch mark, like there had been a fierce fire, but of Eamonn O'Lynn and his Uillean pipes nothing was ever found.

And that is where the true story of Eamonn O'Lynn ends, and the legend of the Drunken Piper who disappeared into the Devil's Churn begins.

Marina Jane

After a storm in the year 1823, a small boat washed up on the sand of Ballygally Bay, five miles north of Larne. Lying in the bottom of the boat was a woman, and in her arms a baby girl, little more than a day old. The woman was dead, but to everyone's great surprise the infant was still breathing. She was taken in by a local woman and, miraculously, not only survived but thrived.

The woman had her baptized and named her Jane, though she was always known as Marina Jane owing to the unusual way she arrived. The woman reared her along with her own family. They sent her to school and church with the local children. But she was always different, and the people never let her forget she was an outsider.

Marina Jane grew into a handsome and capable young woman. She would have made a good and loving wife for any decent young man. In the end she married a neighbouring tenant farmer. No one was surprised. He was a good and gentle soul, a man by the name of John Park. Jane had grown up with John and she had always loved him.

Like many of the men, John went to sea during the leanest months of the year to make ends meet. He could be gone for three months or more, but when he had earned enough to pay the rent he would come home and tend their little farm. By all accounts Jane and John lived quite happily those first two or three years, though Jane never had the child she so longed for.

During one of John's trips Jane had a terrible dream that her beloved husband had been drowned. She was inconsolable. Her closest friends and neighbours tried everything to reason with her, even calling on a local clergyman who declared, "The sea giveth and the sea taketh away." Not surprisingly, Jane took no comfort from his words. Morning, noon and night she could be found walking up and down Ballygally beach with the spent surf breaking around her ankles. She stared out to sea, scanning the horizon for a mast or a sail, but her husband's ship never returned.

Soon the wee farm fell into neglect, and Jane was unable to meet the rent. The bailiffs evicted her. Marina Jane was without a home or so much as a stick of furniture. She remained on the beach at Ballygally to maintain her sad and lonely vigil. With her bare hands she built a cabin from beach stones and driftwood and thatched it with seaweed. Weeks became months and months became years, but never a word of her husband.

If Marina Jane's habits had been peculiar before, now they were unfathomable and to some, unsettling. She was often heard calling out to sea and singing strange laments no one had ever heard before. She seemed to always attract the attention of a seal, drawn in by her mysterious singing, the people supposed. Marina Jane was overheard talking to the animal as if it understood her every word. Around fires all along the coast, fishermen and their wives talked of seals being the reincarnated souls of drowned sailors. They whispered that maybe this seal was Marina Jane's young husband, lost at sea so long ago.

As time passed, people wondered how Marina Jane survived, for she never seemed to forage or fish for her daily needs, meagre as they were. Mischievous locals sometimes spied on her, and she was occasionally seen coming up from the water's edge at low tide in the very early morning with a basket of fish.

"Where did you get those, Jane?" they would ask.

"The sea giveth and the sea taketh away," was all she would ever answer.

Then word began to spread that Marina Jane had been seen cavorting in the sea on a moonlit night with a naked man. Some said they were malicious rumours and the fanciful imaginings of some old gossipmonger with nothing better to do. But then the people noticed that Marina Jane's waist began to swell, and they speculated wildly as to who the father might be. When her time came, they tried to get her into the workhouse to have her child, but she steadfastly refused to go.

When the baby was born, local well-heeled do-gooders with more religion than Christianity had the child taken away from Marina Jane. They said she was not fit to be a mother and that no child should be reared in a hovel such as she lived in, notwithstanding it was no worse than the slum dwellings in the town and a damn sight better than most.

Jane was completely distraught of course. She cut herself off even further from any form of human society. Her hair grew wilder and her clothes more and more ragged. The people said she had lost her mind or had been possessed by some unholy spirit. Some even said she was some class of a witch. But others said she was a soothsayer, gifted with the second sight. Some shunned her out of fear and yet others, usually mothers and wives, would steal down to Jane's cabin at night to beg for news of a loved one away at sea.

Jane would raise a hagstone that hung about her neck on a leather thong. She peered through the hole into the flames of her driftwood fire. She would murmur and mumble and sway back and forth like a shaman. Her eyes rolled back in her head and then eventually, and with great solemnity, she would tell the eager listener that their son or husband or lover was alive and well and would soon return, or that he had passed into the otherworld, as she called it. Sometimes she would convey a comforting or corroborative message from beyond the veil, sometimes not. Invariably Marina Jane's divinations were correct.

Time passed, and by the late 1880s rich sightseers were just beginning to explore the delights of the Glens of Antrim in jaunting cars and charabanc tours out of Larne. The legend of Marina Jane had taken hold and was beginning to spread. She became something of a local curiosity, and someone even made an early photographic plate of her. In it she sat on a rock outside her shack, barefoot and in rags with a strip of cloth tied around her head. She looked for all the world like some exotic native from a far-off land. Who knows, she might well have been, for no one had ever been able to discover from where she came.

In December 1894, another great storm struck. It had been ominously brewing all day and the locals pleaded with Jane to leave her cabin for one night. She refused to go. That afternoon a well-dressed young woman came to Marina Jane's cabin door – little more than a blanket on a rickety frame. Jane searched her face, her gaze flitting from one eye to the other. Without a word passing between them, tears began to trickle down Marina Jane's old leathery face, for this was the child that had been taken away from her. But even the intervention of Marina Jane's long-lost daughter could not persuade her to leave off her vigil for one night.

As the day wore on the sky grew darker and darker and the clouds angrier and angrier, until a fierce wind tore them to tatters and the heavens opened. Rain and hailstones lashed down, and as the waves surged up over the beach wall Marina Jane's cabin was swept away, and her along with it.

She was discovered the next day by a woman gathering driftwood after the storm. Her half-naked body was lying near the water's edge. The woman thought she might still be alive and ran to get help, but when she returned a short time later with some of the menfolk, the body had disappeared. The shoreline was searched for days but no trace of Marina Jane was ever found. In the calm that followed the storm the local people saw two seals rolling and playing in the shallow, peaceful waters of the bay.

Shortly after, the local newspaper printed the picture of Marina Jane, and they published an obituary of sorts, an honour normally reserved for the great and the good. It was remarkable for more than stepping outside the social boundaries of the time. The scant details of Marina Jane's life were recorded, such as anyone remembered. No mention was made of the child that was so cruelly taken away from her by the parish. Bizarrely though, reference was made to Marina Jane's habit of attracting and talking to seals in Ballygally Bay. The writer alluded to the old stories that told of drowned sailors being reincarnated as seals. He even went so far as to say, in a rather derisory tone, that some among the superstitious local peasantry believed that Marina Jane's husband was one such creature, and that he had come from his watery domain to claim her. The piece was branded a sensationalist desecration of the truth and excited much consternation and affront among the more civilised and educated readers of the paper.

In his closing remarks, the author of Marina Jane's unusual obituary referred to the singular nature of her arrival and her mysterious disappearance. He concluded by saying, "in the strange case of Marina Jane Park, or whoever she was, it seems most true that the sea giveth and the sea taketh away."

The Madman's Window

Walk south for about a mile and a half along the coastal path from the village of Glenarm and you will come across a beauty spot known as the Madman's Window. It is a natural rock arch which frames a portal that gives out to the North Channel and the Mull of Kintyre beyond. It looks as though great blocks of white limestone must have been roughly hewn and set in place by the hands of a giant.

Legend has it that a local man, beside himself with grief over the loss of his lover, who, we are told, drowned in the bay, used to sit here and wistfully stare through the opening out across the water until he lost his mind. Different folk will tell you different versions of the story, but this is the right way of it.

Long ago there was a fisherman in the village who had built up a profitable concern. He had a good going clinker–built boat. He had a hundred lobster creels and two long lines of fifty hooks each. After years of hard work, he was at last fit to make a decent living from the sea without having to take on any seasonal farm labour to make ends meet. But he couldn't rest on his laurels, for he never knew when a storm would take some of his gear or the landlord would put his rent up or the price of fish would go down.

One winter he started to knit a net. By the spring it was three yards deep and one hundred yards long. He soon realised he would need some help with it. He took on a young lad from the village, and together they set all one hundred yards of the net in a straight line across the flow of the tide.

The next morning they went out, and as they started to heave on the ropes the weight of the net promised more than they could have hoped for. They got five yards in, ten, fifteen and not a fish, and yet the net felt heavier and heavier. Twenty, twenty-five, thirty yards in, and then they discovered what had been weighing so heavily in the net. It was a gigantic grey seal.

The young lad cursed and reached for the knife. He was about to start slashing and cutting at the seal's fins, but the fisherman stopped him.

"No! Lift its head clear of the water," he ordered.

The animal's eyes were closed. Its body looked lifeless. Then suddenly there was a snuffling and a snorting and a great inhalation of breath. It was alive, but only just. The young lad and the fisherman worked slowly to cut the tangled lines from around the seal's fins and its muzzle. In places the net had cut deeply into its flesh like cheese wire. It was back-breaking work, for the seal was as big as the boat.

When the seal was free of the net, they held it alongside the gunwale of the boat for as long as they could, but eventually they had to let it go. It hung in the water with only its head visible on the surface. Slowly its big dark eyes opened – first one then the other. It looked at the two men in the boat for a long time before slipping beneath the waves.

With the little strength they had left, they gathered in the rest of the net. It was all but destroyed. Wearily they began to row for home. As they did so, every now and then a seal's head broke the surface. It followed the boat until they were safely in over the barmouth of the river and tied up at the quay.

The next morning they went to sea again, for the lobster creels had to be checked and baited and the long lines pulled in and reset. When they began to haul up the creels one by one, again and again they were dumbfounded. On a good day they might have had a dozen decent lobsters but in every creel was a big fine specimen the like of which they had never seen. When they began to pull on the first long line they were nearly beaten, it weighted so heavily. Where they might have had a dozen decent fish on a good day, they had a hundred, and all of them big fine cod the length of a man's arm.

"We'll be rich men if it goes on like this," said the young lad excitedly.

"Aye, but we'll put most of them back," said the fisherman. "Sure we'll let them be caught another day."

And all day they worked, pulling and hauling on the ropes, and every now and then a seal's head broke the surface of the water. It followed them until they were safely in over the barmouth and tied up at the quay.

It was the same the next day and every day after that. Soon the fishmongers were lining the quay to buy their catch. By the end of the season the fisherman had made up all his losses and more.

Well, the fisherman's young helper gave notice that he wanted to see a bit more of the world, and the next tall ship that came into the bay he went aboard her and sailed away. The fisherman let it be known he was looking for another hand, but no one in the village came forward. One day as he was mending creels down by the quay, a young woman approached him.

"I hear," she said, "you are looking for help with the fishing."

The fisherman looked her up and down. She was a stranger, and to his eyes as handsome a young woman as he had ever seen. Her hair was brown and streaked with red and gold like the kelp fronds that grew along the shore in summertime. Her eyes were deep pools and as dark as the night.

"I am," he said, "but let me tell you it's no work for a woman."

"I know as much about the sea and more as any man, and I'm every bit as strong," she said fiercely.

"Is that so?" replied the fisherman, barely able to conceal a laugh. "I suppose it wouldn't cost me anything to let you try your hand."

As it turned out, the young woman was as good as two men, and her knowledge of the sea was second to none. Day about they checked the long lines and then the creels and it was the same every time. A hundred fish, and all of them cod and hake, and a hundred lobsters, and every one a perfect specimen with claws the size of a man's hand. Every day they put half of them back into the sea. When they tied up at the quay fishmongers from Larne and Ballymena were waiting with cart loads of ice, and they bought every fish and every lobster the fisherman landed.

Working side by side every day the fisherman became very fond of the young woman. He began to look upon her as much more than a helping hand. Eventually, he took the courage to speak his mind.

"You know," said he, "you and me – we make a great crew. If I were to ask you to marry me, what would you say?"

The young woman thought only for a moment. "We can be married," she said, "but not churched."

The fisherman accepted her terms, strange as they were. They set up home and lived as husband and wife but were never legally married. Within five years four strong sons came along like steps of stairs, and all of them full of life and laughter. They had their mother's hair and the same dark eyes. The fisherman was as content and happy a man as any could be.

As they approached the seventh anniversary of their first meeting the young woman began to act strangely. She became restless and disagreeable. She awakened in the night and paced the floors. She began to snap at the fisherman for being late or early for his meals or getting the children too excited before bedtime with his carrying on.

The fisherman had often heard of the seven-year itch and one night as they sat by the fire alone, he asked her, "Is everything alright with you? With us?"

She never answered but bid him to follow her down to the water's edge. With the strength of two men, she lifted a huge, flat rock. Under it was a seal's skin.

"Husband," she said, "I must leave you."

The fisherman's heart leapt to his throat. "What? Why must you leave me?"

"The seal who you saved from drowning in your net – he is my father. He is King of the Seal Folk. It is he who has helped you prosper. It is he who sent me to bear your sons to help with the fishing as you grow older. I can only remain on land for seven years. If I stay longer, I can never return to my own kind. I will die."

"But … I love you, and so do the children," said the fisherman.

"And I love you, and them, more than anything, but please understand. I must go. Come to the limestone arch whenever you want me. Call my name and I will answer, day or night."

With that she dropped her clothes on the rocks and donned her seal skin. With one glance over her shoulder, she disappeared into the sea and slipped beneath the waves.

When her clothes were found on the rocks the next morning the villagers began to gossip.

"Poor woman – she must have taken her own life."

"Aye, God love her, there was always a wee want about that lassie," they said.

"And them lovely wee boys are going to be left without a mother. Dear o dear."

When they started to notice that the fisherman went out the shore to the limestone arch every evening and was heard talking to himself as if to his beloved they said, "Poor, poor man. His head's away with grief."

You see, they didn't know the right way of it, so they made up their own story, and that's how the limestone arch got the name of The Madman's Window.

Years later, when the fisherman's family were all up and away, he disappeared himself. Some folk said that he too must have taken his own life. But that's not the right way of it either. I can tell you that he and his seal-wife are living yet, down in the kelp forest where the King of the Seal Folk sits on his throne.

And you may be wondering how on earth I know all this. Well, let's just say I have it on very good authority.

The Whuttrick, the Poacher and the Gamekeeper

Let me begin by explaining the miracle of nature that is the *whuttrick.* It is the small animal otherwise known as the stoat. It is sometimes mistakenly referred to as the weasel, which is similar, but smaller and not found in Ireland. The Irish stoat or, as it is known to country folk in the north of Ireland, the whuttrick, is unique. Its coat rarely turns to white ermine because Irish winters are not sufficiently cold and snowy. And so, it was never hunted here for its pelt.

The whuttrick is a ferocious wee beast. Pound for pound it is far more powerful than the fox and, some would say, far more wily. Being endowed with incredible strength, it can overcome prey ten times its own size. Only about a foot long from nose to tail, its sinuous body can follow anywhere its wee head can squeeze. Even mice in their burrows are not safe. It is completely fearless and as quick as lightening. People rarely get more than a glimpse of it. They are known to possess quite magical powers and can be, by turns, most obliging or very spiteful to humans who interfere in their affairs. Most people round here have the wit to leave them be.

Now the gamekeeper I want you to meet was like so many of his kind. He was a big, ignorant brute of a man. His name was Archibald and he delighted in his authority. You know the type, always willing to go the extra mile to uphold the pettiest law, even at the expense of common sense or compassion.

The poacher who gave him most trouble was a young fella by the name of O'Hara. It should be said O'Hara was by no means an angel. He was the sort of man you could trust with your life, but maybe not your purse. O'Hara poached less out of necessity and more out of devilment. He liked nothing better than to pit himself against Archibald. I say nothing better, but he was just as likely to be found drinking in some tavern or shabeen with a young lady on his knee, as in the field with snare or a slingshot.

Anyway, one afternoon O'Hara was up Glenarm Glen in a place called the High Hollow. He was taking his leisure, it being a fine day and him nursing a sore head from the night before. It could be said he was doing no harm, except that he was trespassing on Lord Antrim's land, and O'Hara never trespassed innocently. He was always on the lookout for the next opportunity to present itself.

As he came through the parkland, he came across a big buck rabbit sitting stock still twenty yards in front of him. It thumped the ground with its hind foot to herald it was alert to danger. Instinctively, O'Hara stopped in his tracks and slowly crouched down. He took a sling shot from his pocket and was just making ready to bowl the rabbit over, when he realised the rabbit was not alarmed by *his* presence, but by that of a whuttrick.

The little assassin boldly approached, and O'Hara held his breath to see what would happen next. He had often heard of the whuttrick's power to entrance its victims but had never seen it for himself. Sure enough, the whuttrick began to perform a dance. It writhed and contorted its body and flicked its tail from side to side. It circled the rabbit seven times, and each time its victim seemed to submit a little more to the charm. The rabbit's eyes grew bigger and bigger and its ears slowly relaxed and flopped down over its back. And all the while the whuttrick came closer and closer as it performed the dance. When it was within striking distance, the whuttrick sunk its needle-sharp teeth into the rabbit's throat. There was no struggle as such, just a slight twitching of the rabbit's hind legs as the life drained out of it.

Just then the whuttrick spied O'Hara. It began a high-pitched whittering and dashing around this way and that, but always coming back to defend its prize. O'Hara laughed out loud with delight at the wee animal's antics.

"I'm not going to rob you of your rabbit," said O'Hara to the whuttrick. "You and me are brothers."

With that the whuttrick took hold of the dead rabbit, many times its own size, and began to drag it away into cover. Just then there was an almighty thump! Everything went black.

A while later O'Hara awoke. There was a lump on the back of his skull the size of a duck egg. His head felt like it was about to burst, and he thought he might have been blinded. He shivered uncontrollably in the darkness. The cold and damp air was heavy with the stench of filth. He could hear water sloshing about in a void beneath him. But where the devil was he? He gathered himself up and took stock of his surroundings. His eyes adjusted to the lack of light and he began to feel around with his hands. There was a door of oak planking bound by iron. The stone walls felt about six feet thick. He was in a prison cell of some kind.

To cut a long story short, O'Hara soon realised there was only one place he could be – somewhere in the bowels of Glenarm Castle. He was right, of course. In fact, he was at the very bottom of a round tower down through which the night soil from the garderobe fell. O'Hara had literally been you-know-what upon from a very great height.

To make matters worse, the sound of water came up from an iron grill in the floor. To his dismay, O'Hara realised that this was sea water which came in with the rising tide and flushed away the accumulated filth twice a day. Even the quick-witted

O'Hara, so used to close shaves and tight corners, despaired at this dire situation. There was nothing left to do but to repent his sins and pray for a mercifully quick end.

As the cold water lapped up around his ankles, he began. "Our Father who art in heaven hallowed be thy name. Thy kingdom come thy will be …" But then he heard a faint scraping at the door. "Who's there?" he cried. "Archibald, is that you? For the love of God, man, let me out."

No answer came. Still the scraping sound reached O'Hara's ears. And then suddenly there was the creak of rusted hinges as the heavy door moved a fraction.

Hardly knowing what had just happened, O'Hara wrenched the door back and ran straight into a stairwell. He bounded up the stone risers three at a time. As he did so, his vision began to come back to him with the first grey light of dawn seeping through window openings above his head. And there skipping before him was the whuttrick. It was leading the way up the stairs and along passageways. At every juncture it made an assured turn and O'Hara followed close behind.

They went through a great kitchen. Slumped in a chair by the big open fire was Archibald, fast asleep with an empty bottle by his side. They saw a rabbit hanging from a meat hook and the whuttrick stopped. It looked up at O'Hara and then at the rabbit. O'Hara knew the little beast meant for him to take it, and as soon as he'd stowed the coney under his coat the whuttrick made off again.

They ran past the dining room and the library and eventually out to the grand entrance hall and the front door. The fire was burning down in the great stone hearth. The whuttrick stopped short of the door. It looked up at O'Hara and then at the fire. O'Hara paused for a moment before he realized what the little creature intended.

"Man, but you're a spiteful one. Is it hanging from the gallows you want to see me?" said O'Hara, and with the fire irons he took the last glowing embers and heaped them on the hall carpet. Then O'Hara turned the key in that mighty door, and he locked it behind him. For good measure he stuck the key in his pocket, and he ran for his life.

Well, he followed that wee whuttrick for miles up the glen and into the wild heather moorland. How far and how long he ran I don't know, but when he couldn't run any further he collapsed and fell fast asleep in a bed of heather.

O'Hara slept so soundly he could have been taken for a man dead to this world. When he started awake the next morning he looked for the whuttrick, but it was nowhere to be seen. He felt his head and there was the nasty remains of a painful bump. Then he remembered the rabbit, but when he reached inside his coat there was nothing there. So strange were the events as they came to back to his mind, he began to think it was, after all, only a strange, strange dream.

As he rolled over in the heather, something hard and jagged pushed into his ribs. He felt for it to restore his comfort, and that's when he found the big iron front door key of Glenarm Castle. O'Hara kept it for the rest of his long days and only very occasionally took it out to remind himself of his adventure with the whuttrick.

Whether O'Hara repented his shameful deeds I cannot say, for these events took place a very long time ago. But it is well documented that the old Glenarm Castle was destroyed by a fire. An explanation as to how the blaze started, or if anyone was injured, was not recorded. A new castle was built on the other side of Glenarm River. And there a castle stands on the same site to this day.

Very likely they have all manner of modern accoutrements to detect the slightest whiff of smoke. Even so, the present Lord Antrim would do well to make sure his gamekeeper does not cross the whuttricks that still live in Glenarm Glen.

A Poacher Turned Stick-Maker

Let me introduce you a man called John Mor Magill. He was poacher of salmon and pheasants and hares. A hundred years ago and more he was the bane of gamekeepers and bailiffs up and down the Glens of Antrim, but they never caught him.

One day, in the month of November, he was up in the top reaches of his native glen. Over his back were slung four or five big hares, and between them and his old muzzle-loading gun, he was heavily weighed down and ready for home. He stopped to rest by Glenarm River at a pool they called the Salmon Leap, from where he had taken many a fish just below the waterfall that tumbles into it.

As his eyes fell upon the surface of the brown water, John spied the distinct shadow of a gigantic salmon. It was lying in close to the bank. "That fish is forty-five-pound weight if it's an ounce," he said to himself. "And by God it's four foot long if it's an inch." John Mor was breathless with sheer excitement.

From side to side the fish's mighty tail slowly beat the current, and it took great gulps of the white water churned up by the falls. John Mor could hardly believe his eyes. It was by far and away the biggest salmon he had ever seen or heard tell of.

As the desire to take this salmon overcame John Mor, he cursed his luck for not having a gaff or a net with him. He was loathe to leave the fish, for he knew it might be gone before he could return. Being ill-equipped as he was, he had no choice but leave it. Then a lightning flash of pure inspiration came to him. "I'll shoot the bloody thing!" he said to himself.

He reached into his ammunition pouch for a lead ball, but damn-it-all, wasn't it empty. He was completely out of shot and, it seemed, out of luck. But then he had another bright idea. He didn't have to look too hard or too far till he found a blackthorn tree. On its spiky branches some autumn fruit still hung – sloe berries, black and shiny like miniature plums, and as bitter as gall.

He plucked one from the tree and shoved it into his mouth. Lord of all goodness, but it was sour. His face screwed up like a prune while he sucked the flesh off the stone and spat it out. And there it was, the perfect size for his gun, and as round and hard as a marble. He poured a drop of black powder down the barrel, dropped in the sloe stone and rammed a wad home to hold everything in place. Then he pulled the hammer back. Half-cock, full-cock. He took aim and squeezed the trigger. There was a great flash and a thunderclap. A cloud of black smoke filled the air and hung in the trees.

The sloe stone struck the poor salmon fair and square in the middle of its broad back. The fish took off, jumping and buck-leaping up and down. It thrashed its big tail until the water was whipped into a frothing, swirling whirlpool. And then with a mighty leap, it cleared the waterfall in one go and disappeared up the river.

John Mor spent the rest of the day and all the next looking for his fish, but he never saw it again. That salmon became the stuff of legend. It was the greatest one-that-got-away story ever told. As time went by it got bigger and heavier as people began to add length and weight to the salmon, but John Mor's version of events never varied.

Well, time nor tide wait for no man, and the years passed. John Mor's bones began to creak and ache, and his joints stiffened. He eventually hung up his old muzzle-loading gun along with his fishing nets and his snares. He had to content himself with dreaming about past glories and telling tales about the salmon and the hares and the pheasants that he had poached in his youth. And, like so many older men of his class and creed, John Mor took up the gentle and patient art of stick-making.

He would go out of an autumn day and cut hazel and blackthorn saplings and let them season for a year or two. Then he would dress them, and maybe carve their handles into the shape of a leaping salmon or a pheasant's head. Then he would give them a wee lick of varnish and take them down to the tavern or the fair, where he sold them for a few shillings.

One November day, John Mor was up in the glen cutting sticks. Just for reminiscence's sake he sat down by the pool they called the Salmon Leap. While he was smoking his pipe, he noticed a blackthorn tree growing out from the edge of the bank. It was eight foot high, thick as a brush shaft and just as straight. "That would make a quare shillelagh or maybe even two," John thought to himself, and following the wisdom of an old Irish country proverb that says, *if you see a stick, cut it*, John Mor stepped forward. Taking hold of the tree, he bent down to take it off by the root with his bill hook.

Well, the bush gave a quiver and then it began to shake. "Bejaper's, that's an odd thing," thought John to himself. The next moment the tree took off, and him holding onto it for dear life. Round and round that pool it went, and when John Mor looked down, wasn't the blackthorn tree growing out the back of a giant salmon and him standing on it. It was a hundred and fifty pounds if it was an ounce, and eight foot long if it was an inch. John realised it was the very same fish he had shot with the sloe stone all those years before.

It went up the pool and back down a dozen times. Then with one mighty swish of its tail it cleared the waterfall and was away up the river faster than a galloping horse, and John still holding on for dear life. Next thing John could see they were fast approaching a stone bridge. Instinctively, he ducked down, but it was too late for the salmon. The minute it went in below the bridge, didn't it get stuck and John still standing on its back. Well, it thrashed about till it was exhausted, but with its belly in the gravel of the riverbed and the top of that blackthorn tree jammed in below the bridge it could neither go forward nor back.

Once John Mor caught his breath, he looked at that mighty salmon and he looked at the blackthorn growing out of its back, and he wondered to himself what he should do. And do you know what he done? He jumped down into the water up to his knees, and with his billhook he hacked that thorn stick clean away from the salmon's back. When the fish was free it took off like a bullet from a gun, leaving nothing but foam and spray in its wake.

John Mor took his blackthorn home. When it was well seasoned, he dressed it and made a fine walking stick out of it. And the fact is that most people don't believe that story, but you can take it from me that it's absolutely true in every particular. You see, John Mor Magill passed that stick on, along with the story, to the man who passed them on to the man who passed them on to me.

And now I've just passed the story on to you, but the stick that John Mor Magill cut from that salmon's back, well, I hope you'll understand that I want to hold onto it, for I might need it myself one day.

Away with the Faeries

Archie and Paddy McCallion were twin brothers. They were born with great tufts of red hair and twinkling sapphire-blue eyes. The youngest of twelve siblings, they were as lively a pair of wee boys as you could imagine.

The family lived in a clachan called Straidkilly – a wee gathering of half a dozen houses halfway along the three miles of old back road between the village of Glenarm and Carnlough. Like their neighbours, the McCallions were poor enough and only just scratched a living from the few hungry acres they farmed. The braes that swept up to the Antrim Plateau and the rough fields around Straidkilly were riven by deep crevices here and there where the limestone cracked and fractured as it slipped down over the underlying clay. Occasionally there were sudden slides, but usually the land just crept inch by imperceptible inch towards the sea.

As a result, the landscape was treacherous. Wandering sheep and cattle sometimes came to grief by disappearing into the earth, never to be seen or heard tell of again. Around the hearth fires at night local children were warned about the wee folk who lived deep down in the crevices, and who were always on the lookout for little boys and girls to kidnap and take to the otherworld. The stories seemed to have the desired effect, and most children with any wit steered well clear.

Now for the first six or seven years of Archie and Paddy's lives they were inseparable and even their mother had trouble telling them apart, so alike were they. But then a strange thing happened. Archie disappeared! His mother said, "He was there one minute and gone the next!" They searched for him high up and low down. Lanterns were shone down into the inky crevices, and brave men were lowered on ropes into the bigger caverns. After a month of searching night and day not a trace of Archie was found.

"God love wee Archie," the people said. "He must have wandered off and fallen into a hole in the ground." His body would never be found now. His poor mother would have to mourn his loss for the rest of her days, and no grave to tend.

But slowly Mrs McCallion began to dry her tears. She had the other children to care for, but Archie had been the youngest. Along with his brother Paddy they had been the family favourites. Now that Archie was gone Paddy was the sole beneficiary of the family's love and attention. He got whatever he wanted, and good manners were never put into him. In fact, he was spoiled rotten. Blinded by her sorrow over Archie, Mrs McCallion could not see that she was ruining his older twin brother. She barely let Paddy out of her sight. He could do no wrong and when the other children or anyone else complained that he did, Mrs McCallion would defend him to the hilt. "Would you ever give Paddy peace," she would say. "Isn't he still pining for his brother. Poor wee angel." And slowly but surely Paddy the "wee angel" turned into a wee devil.

Then a year to the day that Archie had disappeared, Mrs McCallion was milking a goat out in the yard. Paddy was tied to her with a length of twine, and him sucking and chewing contentedly on a big toffee apple. Just then a strange thing happened – Archie reappeared! He sauntered around the gable end of the house as if he had only been gone a minute or two. His mother ran for him, dragging Paddy off his feet and over the cobbles, screeching and bawling.

"Oh Archie, Archie, Archie," she cried. "It's a miracle. You've come back to us alive!" And she hugged and kissed her long-lost young son like a woman possessed.

Well, they quizzed and questioned Archie as to where he had been and how he had survived all that time without food or water, but not a word could they get out of him. He had been struck dumb. His clothes were exactly as he had worn them on the day of his disappearance, and there was not even a hair on his head out of place. A doctor was called for, who pronounced Archie quite healthy and showing no signs of distress. The priest said, "The Lord works in mysterious ways." But the people began to whisper that Archie had been "away with the faeries."

From that day on, Archie became the centre of his mother's attention and Paddy's nose was pushed out of joint. If Paddy so much as looked at Archie the wrong way his mother would chastise him severely. "Don't you dare upset your wee brother. You know he's not right since he came back," she would say. Now if Paddy threw a temper tantrum, he was apt to get a clip around the ear and sent to bed with no supper.

Anyway, another year passed, and Archie began to speak, slowly at first like a baby, but eventually his full powers of speech came back to him. Strangely though, his growth had been stunted and now Paddy was a good three inches taller and much sturdier than his once identical twin brother.

As Archie began to talk more, he was able to tell his family about the wee folk with whom he had spent "only one night", as he said. Archie seemed to have no way to fathom that he had been gone away for a year. He said he had refused all the strange-looking food and drink they had offered him and that he had cried himself to sleep calling for his mammy.

If Archie had been the blue-eyed boy before, his mother completely doted on him now. No matter what silly, childish pranks Archie got up to, it was never his fault. "That's the faeries making my wee angel misbehave," his mother would always say. But when Paddy played up, she would call, "Patrick McCallion, you're one wee spoiled brat!" and she would take a sally rod and beat him. And that's the way their lives went. Archie remained the apple of his mother's eye, and Paddy was slowly turned into the black sheep of the family.

Once upon a time, Archie and Paddy had been joined at the hip; now they were strangers to one another. And not only that, but they were also as different as day and night. Archie had grown slowly, never reaching more than five foot in height and was always very slight of build. Paddy had grown into a fine big lump of a youth, and more ill-set with every year that passed. By the time they were fully-fledged men, Paddy was a good foot or more taller than his brother, and compared to wee Archie, he was as strong as a bull. Their natures differed too. Archie kept himself to himself. As the people said, "he was as odd as tae", but they liked him well enough, for although he was distant, he was always very civil. Paddy, on the other hand, was a more boisterous character, and the people hated to see him coming. He was full of himself and foul-mouthed, and when he was drunk, which was often, he was bullish and unbearable.

Time passed, and the rest of the McCallion family married and went their separate ways. Archie and Paddy's parents eventually passed on and the twin brothers were left in the wee crumbling farmhouse alone. By now they could barely look at one another, never mind speak. Apart from sleeping under the one roof their paths did not cross. Archie inclined towards the village of Glenarm for all his needs and Paddy to Carnlough.

Archie lived by labouring to local farmers and was known as a good and honest worker. He went to mass on Sundays and only took a drink or maybe two on a Saturday night. Paddy, on the other hand, had the name of being lazy and untrustworthy.

His reputation was well deserved, though people were unaware to what depths he could stoop.

Paddy stole eggs from henhouses and, for spite, left stones in their place. He made hay and sold it to a local horse dealer, then he would creep back under cover of darkness and steal a few bails here and there and sell it back to his unwitting victim until he had doubled his money. He lifted potatoes out of the drills from his neighbour's fields, and when he sold them to unwary housewives, he half-filled the bags with soil.

It wasn't that he amassed any great fortune of money from his skulduggery, for he drunk every penny he done his neighbours out of. He just seemed to take great delight in cheating people and being mischievous. For pure badness he took boats from Glenarm River and poached salmon in the bay, leaving fish scales and guts everywhere as evidence, and the bailiffs seized more than one innocent man's boat. He crept into byres at night and milked cows dry. He helped himself to peat from his neighbour's turf stacks, burned down their haysheds and fouled in their wells. Then he would stand at the bar of public houses holding court and holding forth. "It's them faeries is to blame," he would say. "You couldn't watch them. They're always up to no good. Sure, didn't they take my own brother one time? And he never has been the better of it."

Well, if you throw enough muck some of it will stick, and the people started to believe Paddy McCallion. "The faeries are out of hand entirely," they said. "Something will have to be done about them." And then ancient faerie thorns began to get damaged and cut down, horseshoes were thrown into the cracks and crevices all around Straidkilly, for everyone knew the faeries could be driven away by their fear of iron! The priest even came one Sunday. He sprinkled holy water everywhere and placed a curse on the faerie folk. All-out war was declared. And all the while only one man knew what was really afoot, and that was Paddy McCallion, for of course he was behind all the rascality.

One Saturday evening late in the year, Archie was in Glenarm village as usual, and Paddy was in Carnlough. Archie stayed in the pub later than normal, for the company was good and a homely fire burned in the hearth. In those days, favourite and inoffensive patrons like Archie could stay well beyond the legal closing time at the publican's pleasure and the peelers never bothered them much. Eventually, however, Archie took the road for home, which was only a walk of a mile and half. There was a full moon, so the way was well lit, which was fortunate, for Archie was well lit too. Unsteady as he was on his feet, he managed to make it home without mishap, almost.

As he was passing a barn on the opposite side of the road from his own lane, he heard voices raised in glee and the sound of a fiddler. "That's strange," he thought to himself, and under different circumstances he might have scurried on home, but emboldened by the drink, Archie decided to investigate. He crept closer, keeping to the shadows, and peeked in through a knothole in the timbers of the barn. What he saw sent the shivers down his wee wiry spine, for there was his brother Paddy surrounded by wee folk drinking and ceilidhing for all they were worth. One wee fella was tearing away at a fiddle playing the fastest, most melodious reels ever heard. Archie even recognised one of the faeries from the time they had tried to keep him all those years before. He seemed to be their leader, for he was the only one that spoke.

Paddy was taking great gulps of liquor from a tumbler. Archie felt a powerful urge to burst in and warn him against it, but they hadn't spoken in years, and anyway it was probably too late.

"So tell us this, Paddy, was it you that stole the lead of the chapel roof and sold it to the tinkers?" asked the faerie chief.

"It was, surely," said Paddy, laughing out loud. "And I'll tell ye better than that – it was me put the peelers on to them and got them the blame … it was me set fire to their oul caravan for good measure!"

This admission brought great guffaws of laughter from all assembled.

"You did not? Man, dear you're a holy terror, Paddy McCallion," said the wee faerie.

"I did so," said Paddy, "and I did a lot more besides."

With great pleasure Paddy poured forth a whole litany of crimes and wrongdoings for which he was the proud culprit. At each confession the wee folk cheered and guffawed, encouraging him to even more scandalous disclosures. By the time Paddy had divulged all his misdeeds he was roaring drunk, but still the wee folk filled and refilled his tumbler. Archie was dumbfounded and disgusted in equal measure. Low as his opinion of Paddy was, never in a million years did he think such wickedness was within the grasp of someone as closely related to him as his very own twin brother.

As Archie looked on, Paddy said at last, "And do you see that wee hateful brother o mine." Paddy's speech was slurred, and his mouth twisted horribly as the venom in his words came out. "Some of these days I'm going to throw that wee devil down a hollow and they'll never find him!"

At that the head faerie turned around and looked directly into Archie's eye peering in through the knothole. Knowing well that Archie was there watching and listening all along, he raised an eyebrow as if to say, "What d'ye think of that, ye boy ye?"

Shaking with anger and dismay, Archie withdrew. That whole night he lay on his bed with his boots on and the fire iron in his hand for fear that Paddy or the faeries would come for him. Not a wink of sleep did he get. By dawn he was ready to confront his brother, but Paddy was nowhere to be found.

Eventually Archie went to the barn where he had eavesdropped the night before. And there was Paddy slumped in a corner, his head hanging down on his chest and the slavers dripping from his chin.

"Brother! You better wake up for I have a crow to pluck with you!" Archie called, but Paddy never moved. As Archie came closer, he could see that his brother was not sleeping at all. Paddy was as dead as a door nail.

Well to cut a long story short, the peelers were summoned. Archie said he had been the last person to see his brother alive, and he reached a big polis sergeant two pages of a note in which Paddy confessed to all his misdeeds, in every detail. It was signed in a rather indistinct and unsteady hand, *Patrick McCallion*. Never before in the records of the Royal Irish Constabulary had so many unsolved crimes been cleared in one fell swoop.

Of course the big sergeant was delighted, for he could take all the credit. Whether he ever suspected that Archie had forged the note I couldn't tell you, but it didn't matter, for there were no other witnesses or evidence in the case.

In his official report the policeman recorded: "Patrick McCallion, most likely suffering from a guilty conscience, wrote and signed a detailed confession of his many crimes and then proceeded to poison himself by consuming a large amount of poitín, the source of which has yet to be established."

The tragic incident was quietly written off, as the sergeant said, "to spare the McCallion family name as much as possible."

The local people were left to make sense of the strange events at their leisure, and things quickly settled down. But then the people began to put two and two together and all fingers were pointed at Paddy McCallion. He had been the mischief maker all along! Archie was never directly tarred with the same brush, but he could feel people were mistrustful of him. As time passed and there were no more late-night shenanigans in the parish, people began to leave their doors open at night again. They left the faerie thorns well enough alone too and they quit throwing horseshoes down the cracks and crevices in the ground. Peace and harmony returned to Straidkilly once more.

Only Archie, the boy that was once away with faeries, knew the whole story, and he never spoke to a single person about it, except for that big polis sergeant to whom he told everything – almost everything.

When Archie disappeared years later the people sighed and said, "Dear, dear, what an unfortunate pair of boys them McCallion twins were." Very few people ever entertained the idea that Archie was away with the faeries again – even fewer that this time he had gone of his own free will.

The Last Wolf

In the year 1712 a journey through the Glens of Antrim was a dangerous undertaking. There was no coast road in those days, just a rough track. There were thickly wooded braes in which an unwary traveller could easily become lost. In among the hazel and the rowan, the birch and the oak, lurked banshees and faeries. There were bands of cut-throat robbers, wild boar and packs of hungry wolves. It was a brave man, or a foolhardy one, that would venture into that part of the country alone. It was said not even priests were safe.

Nevertheless, a certain clergyman prayed for divine protection and mounted on a pony he set out on a pilgrimage. He travelled from his native parish on the north coast, down through the Glens of Antrim heading for the burial shrine of Saint Patrick in the County Down.

As he neared the little village of Carnlough he saw a wind-carved limestone pillar the locals still call the White Lady. The road swept up the hillside away from the shore. The woods became very thick and the way narrow.

After about a mile the priest could see that the path up ahead diverged. To the left it turned back down towards the sea. To the right it rose up towards Nappin Mountain. When he reached the forkings his pony stopped dead in its tracks. The priest tried to spur him on to the left-hand path, but the animal refused. He tried harder. It refused again. He was about to flog the animal when he heard the bone-chilling sound of a howling wolf – Awhoooo!

Without waiting for his master, the pony took to the right-hand path. And then, from out of the undergrowth stepped a huge grey wolf with wild green eyes. It blocked the narrow path, and again the pony stopped dead in its tracks. Slowly the wolf approached, and the pony began to rear up almost dislodging its rider.

"Whoa, whoa there," said a deep, commanding voice. The priest looked about but could see no one. His pony settled, and when the priest looked again the wolf was six feet in front staring him straight in the eye.

"Father, do not be afraid. I mean you no harm," it said.

"What trickery is this?" said the priest. And he held up a crucifix, saying, "Begone, Satan."

"Fear not, Father. All is not what it seems. I am neither a wolf nor a devil."

"Then in the name of God what are you?"

"I am a man in wolf's clothing, Father. Many years ago my people were cursed. Every seven years since then a young man and a young woman have been cast out to wander the land in the form of wolves. If they survive, bearing in mind that one year as a wolf is seven years as a man, they may return to die in their beds, and two others must take their place."

"And if they do not survive?" the priest asked, his curiosity outweighing his fear.

"Many have not returned, but in over twelve hundred years it has never happened that both the man and woman have perished during their exile. When that happens, the curse will be lifted."

"And what in heaven's name do you want of a poor holy man like me?" asked the priest.

"My companion is dying, Father. She is my beloved wife, and it is her wish that in her final hours she receive the holy sacrament of the Last Rights. Do this, and I give you my word that I will guide you back to safety and you may carry on with your journey."

"And if I refuse?" said the priest.

The man-wolf looked up to the darkening sky and said wearily, "Time is short, Father. We must hurry. Follow me and I will take you to my wife."

With little choice, the priest anxiously followed. The wolf led them to a giant, ancient oak tree, the bowl of which was hollowed out. Inside lay a she-wolf, moaning and sighing heavily like any human in mortal distress. When she saw the priest, human tears trickled down the fur of her muzzle. The priest began to perform the ritual right up to the point of the last Holy Communion.

When he hesitated the she-wolf spoke, "I beg you, Father, complete your duty and give me the viaticum."

The priest demurred saying, "I do not have it with me."

At that the man-wolf raised his hackles and showed his fearsome canine teeth. A deep growl rose in his throat. "You forget yourself, Father," it said. "The consecrated hosts are in a leather pouch that hangs about your neck."

With a trembling hand the priest offered the she-wolf the communion wafer. She accepted the sacrament as devoutly as any Christian woman on her death bed, and then she lay down her head once more.

Inside that oak tree, the priest and the two wolves spent what remained of that short night. Certain that the man-wolf meant to devour him, the priest never slept, not even for a moment. He prayed continuously, saying the Rosary over and over again. Just before dawn the she-wolf breathed her last. Her mate raised his mighty head and howled for a long, long time – Awhoooo! Then he wept like a child, and even in the throes of his terrible fear the priest felt some pity for the creature.

With a great sigh, the man-wolf gathered himself and he led the priest some distance through the woods and across the heather of Nappin Mountain. They reached a ravine where the Cranny River tumbles down off the plateau. They followed a steep path, and at the bottom of a narrow waterfall over-hung with trees and ferns, the wolf stopped.

"I must take my rest here," he said. "I have kept my word, Father. Now you may go in peace. Follow the stream down to the sea and you will find the village of Carnlough."

"I will tell no man what I have seen and done this past night," said the priest. And then he solemnly blessed the animal. "In nomine Patris et Filii et Spiritus Sancti. Amen."

He rode off down the rough track as quickly as he could, peering over his shoulder often, for fear he would be attacked the moment his back was turned. But the wolf had lain down beside the pool at the foot of Cranny Falls.

When the priest got to the village he told all and sundry how he had been attacked and described the exact spot where he had last seen the wolf. A band of men armed themselves with cudgels and muskets and, led by a great grey-coated hound straining on a rope, they set off up the track to Cranny Falls. And there by the side of the pool they found a huge dog-wolf, lying just as the priest had said.

"Is it sleeping?" one of the men whispered. Another raised a musket and fired a lead ball into its side. The wolf heaved one last merciful sigh, and a twelve-hundred-year-old curse was lifted.

The men carried the wolf's great body back down to the village in triumph for everyone to gaze upon in fear and wonderment, and to claim the bounty of a few silver shillings from Lord Antrim's agent. Cranny Waterfall above the village of Carnlough was entered into the annals of local history as the last place in the Glens of Antrim a native Irish wolf was seen or heard tell of. As for the priest, his name was not recorded.

The Last Man

I'm the last man cutting turf up on Capanagh Bog
And it won't be long before I'll be pushing up the sod.
When I go, there won't be one to step into my boots,
For my sons are in America putting down new roots.

They say I'm far too old to be up here on my own,
But a hard-working country life is all I've ever known.
Making hay and reaping corn was a blessing not a curse,
Autumn days gathering spuds and bringing home the turf.

"All that hard work?" young folk say, "and not a thing to show
But calloused hands and midgey bites and a ruddy wind-burnt
    glow."
But if I had my time all over, I'd do the very same again.
I'd still go up to Capanagh with my barrow and my sleán.

Against all wind and weather in springtime down the years
I'd brave the cold drip at my nose, sleet blowing round me ears.
It was a small, small price to pay to hear the curlew call
And the lapwing and the skylark and the cuckoo best of all.

There was grouse and hares aplenty and wee, green-jewelled
    frogs
And cotton grass and myrtle and all the flowers of the bog.
There was fairy flax and heather and sweet forget-me-nots

And golden spikes of asphodel to brighten up the moss.

Gaily coloured dragonflies with silver whispering wings
And big fat hairy caterpillars, no end of wondrous things.
And we took it all for granted, no fear for nature then.
We never thought a way of life was coming to an end.

But I'm the last man cutting turf up on Capanagh Bog,
A relic from a bygone age like a Banshee out in the fog.
They're welcome to their gas and oil and cheap electric light.
There's no company like an open fire on the darkest winter's
    night.

Now they say that cutting turf destroys the environment,
But them that wrought the bog by hand barely made a dent.
Seasons turned and lives went by lit by the peat fire's flame.
Little harm was ever done by the barrow and the sleán.

The old boys that I once knew walked lightly on this earth,
They had a real love for the bog and knew what it was worth,
They had a name for every bird from the linnet to the snipe,
And the wisest always took the time to stop and smoke a pipe.

Nowadays it's not for want of fuel I come up here.
I could heat myself with firewood for it's not so very dear.
I come up here to clear my mind for tranquillity is bliss,
To cut my turf for old time's sake and of course to reminisce.

About my father and my uncles, my brothers Sean and Hugh
And all the neighbour folk of old from the townland of
    Loughdoo.
Sometimes I hear their voices and I answer with a laugh,
For in my mind I'm back there to the days we used to have.

Time was that every country man worked his bank of peat
And turf provided everything from work to light and heat.
All summer long we'd foot the turf and build the castles higher,
To dry the peats and get them home and stack them for the fire.

The earthy smell of fresh peat smoke always takes me back,
To my mother baking soda bread, the stories and the craic.
The cups of tae and fiddlers, the big kettle on the boil.
It always seemed well worth it then, the long days and the toil.

Now the birds are not so plentiful, and you'd hardly see a hare,
The peat banks are overgrown and there's rushes everywhere.
There's nobody comes up here now but me and my old dog,
For I'm the last man cutting turf up on Capanagh Bog.

The Farmer's Bull

There was once a Glens of Antrim farmer by the name of Paddy McCloy. He didn't have much in the way of land or wealth, and he had far less in the way of inclination or wherewithal to get more. He was a man of very simple philosophy and sharp wit. Regarding mortality, he was often heard to say, "Eat plenty, drink plenty and smoke plenty, and you'll live. And sure if you dinnae, you'll die."

Of one long-standing spinster woman who surprised everyone by agreeing to marry a neighbouring farmer he commented, "Ah weel, she'll naw tear in the plucking anyway."

Paddy himself had never been married. Asked about his feelings toward an unattractive widow woman who had an eye for him he said, "I'd be hard up for an apple when I would ate an onion."

Paddy was a man of faultless wisdom, no doubt, but he was also a creature of very strange habits. Every evening all through the spring and summertime Paddy put a rooster under a bucket on the window ledge by his bed. He propped up the vessel with a bit of turf – just enough that the morning light could get in so that the rooster would crow at dawn, and by such means made sure he never over-slept.

In the wintertime he went down to the river every morning and stood with his feet in the icy water until they were blue with the cold. Then he would pull on what was left of his holey woollen stockings and slip his freezing feet into his hob-nailed boots. He swore that even in the chilliest of weather this procedure kept his feet as warm as toast for the rest of the day.

Summer *or* winter, Paddy wore his hob-nailed boots day and night. When he eventually lay down to rest each evening, he did so with boots still laced and a greatcoat buttoned up around his neck. "Ye never know when the bailiffs might come," he used to say.

Paddy farmed little more than two or three rough acres – "all sprits and whins," (rushes and gorse) as the folk used to say. He kept a few laying hens, and half a dozen ducks. There was always a half-bred Ulster sow in the yard and a goat or two for a drop of milk, but the pride of all his stock was a wee red Dexter bull.

He was always referred to as The Bull. He had a ring through his nose – more for decoration than anything else. It was never needed, for he was as quiet as a mouse. All summer long The Bull had the run of the low meadow. In the wintertime he was stalled in the byre and fed on the best of good, sweet summer hay. Paddy brushed him near every day and washed him on Saturdays, as if he was getting him ready for a show. No expense was ever spared to spoil The Bull. Paddy and his prize Dexter were the talk of the countryside.

One day a neighbouring farmer met Paddy and asked, "Is there any chance I could get the services of The Bull for a wee heifer I hae?"

"Certainly," said Paddy.

When the job was done the neighbour said, "Thanks very much, Paddy." And away he went.

Well, first in ones and then in droves, farmers for miles around who kept a Dexter cow called with Paddy to ask for the services of The Bull. Down the lane they came, rope in hand, walking their cows, meaning to get them in calf. And when the job was done, they would call over their shoulders,

"Thanks very much Paddy," and lead their cows out the lane and away back to wherever they had come from. Not a single one among them ever thought it worth their while to ask Paddy if he needed a penny for the service of his bull. They took it for granted that since the boy before had got the use of The Bull for free then they would too. And so, it went on and on and on.

Well, Paddy was a kindly, neighbourly sort of a boy with a gentle soul belying his wry wit and strange ways. Still and all, he began to get fed up with being taken for granted. One day the local thatcher was mending a bit of a leak on Paddy's roof and when the job was done Paddy said, "Thanks very much," and made to walk away.

"I need more than a 'thanks very much,'" said the thatcher. "The wife would take a quare look at me if I worked all week and came home without a penny to show for it, or a bite for the table."

It was the same with the blacksmith when Paddy went to get a cartwheel re-shod.

"Are you mad, Paddy?" he roared. "How would you expect me to feed my weans and pay my rent if all I ever got was a 'thanks very much?'"

When he went to the doctor to get a boil lanced or the butcher for half a pound of sausages, they just shook their heads at him and said the same thing. Paddy felt like a fool, so he went to his clergy man to broach the matter. He explained how the farmers roundabout never offered him a ha'penny for the services of The Bull.

"If I had a shilling for every farmer that said 'thanks very much' I'd be a rich man, Father."

"Yes," said the priest, "but scripture tells us to love thy neighbour, Paddy. Man does not live on bread alone, you know."

"Naw, indeed, Father, but he'll no live lang withoot it either!"

And Paddy went away home feeling even more aggrieved than before. When he went out that night to fodder The Bull there wasn't a single sheaf of hay left in the barn. The Bull would have to go hungry.

The next day another farmer arrived looking for a cow serviced.

"Thanks very much, Paddy," said the farmer and away he went.

It was the same the next day and the next, but without any fodder for The Bull and not a ha'penny to buy any, the poor animal began to weaken and fall into bad health. Eventually, one day a farmer came with a cow on a halter and The Bull was brought out into the yard, but he showed not the slightest bit of interest in her.

"Maybe she's no ready yet. You may bring her back another day," said Paddy.

The farmer raged. "I've better things to do with my time than come here on a fool's errand and your baiste not fit to do the job."

Paddy just shrugged his shoulders, and the farmer stamped away ranting and raving.

Soon after that another farmer came with a cow, but Paddy had sad news for him.

"You've wasted your time the day," he said.

"Why's that?" said the farmer.

"The Bull is dead."

"Dead?"

"Aye, he's stiff as a boord."

"What kilt him?" said the farmer, fearing now for his own animal's welfare. "Was it TB or foot and mouth or what was it?"

"Naw," said Paddy, "It was 'thanks very much' that kilt him."

And that's how an old country saying was born. You see, after that whenever anyone asked for or accepted a favour or a service and offered only thanks in return, it was often muttered under the offended party's breath.

"Aye, 'thanks very much.' That's what kilt the farmers bull."

The Wreck of the Enterprise of Lynn

Ringfad is a small, rocky reef that shelters a little sandy bay just north of the village of Carnlough. Generations of local young people have learned to swim in the shallow water there. It is a good place too for gathering dulse (edible seaweed) and whullocks (whelks). On a calm summer morning when the tide is out and the sun is glinting on the surface of the sea, it is hard to imagine the terrible events that took place here almost two hundred years ago.

On New Years' Day in the year 1827, a rich West Indiaman by the name of the *Enterprise of Lynn*, laden with precious cargo, set sail from Rio de Janeiro bound for Liverpool. On board was a crew of twenty-odd souls including Captain J. Bond and his good lady wife, their children and an unrelated passenger who happened to be the President of Chile's son, no less. He had taken passage to England.

The captain's wife had sailed with her husband many times before and was always beloved of his crew. She was no idle passenger. She could plot a course and use a sextant. She could read charts and navigate by the stars. She had steered the *Enterprise of Lynn* from Valparaiso around Cape Horn, one of the most dangerous stretches of water known to mariners.

Superstitious as they were, the crew regarded her as something of a good luck charm. And when they set out on the six and a half thousand miles of open ocean between Rio de Janeiro and their home port of Liverpool, not a single man on board had any doubts that they would get home safe and sound.

They sailed up through the Atlantic Ocean and crossed the equator. They put in briefly at Tenerife in the Canaries Islands to take on provisions. And after two months of hard sailing the boy in the crow's nest shouted, "Land ho! Two points off the starboard bow!"

The land he saw was the rugged and treacherous southwest coast of Ireland. They still had a long way to go, but the cooler climes were welcome and the predictable winds pushed them onwards. Their confidence was well founded.

Up around Rathlin Island and down into the Sea of Moyle they sailed, with the Mull of Kintyre on their portside and the Glens of Antrim on their starboard. And then, on the evening of the 3rd of March, less than one day out of Liverpool, a gale blew up in the Irish Sea. It was as ferocious as anything they had encountered off Cape Horn. As they hugged the Irish coast the captain's wife consulted her charts. She knew exactly where they were, for she had taken a sighting at noon that day. She was heading for the only safe anchorage on that part of the coast – Glenarm Bay.

To starboard the hills were coated with snow right down to sea level. In the blizzard conditions, visibility was desperately poor. Every now and again the crew caught glimpses of faint lights from the shore side cottages which gave them great heart. But with only three or four miles between the *Enterprise of Lynn* and the safety of Glenarm Bay, tragedy struck. She ran aground on the rocks of Ringfad. The ship was less than thirty yards from shore, but it was only a matter of time before the pounding surf would smash her timbers to smithereens. At least eleven of the crew were lost, including the captain and his wife. The President of Chile's son also entered the raging sea, never to see dry land again.

The poor peasants from all along the Largy Shore left their firesides. They came to render what little assistance they could, and hoping too that there might be some goods to be salvaged into the bargain – a barrel of brandy or a plank or two of wood.

For years it had been the custom for mariners to wear gold and silver rings on their fingers and in their ears. The jewellery was engraved with their names and their home ports in the hope that if they drowned or otherwise died at sea, the value of the precious metal might be enough to have their remains returned to their loved ones – for all sailors shiver at the thought of being buried at sea.

When the local people found dead and dying sailors bejewelled with gold and silver and the handsomely dressed officers, they were seized by a wild hunger. They set to work hacking off fingers and ears to take possession of the riches before their neighbours. Fights broke out over who had a better claim. They became like a pack of wolves bickering over a carcass.

As dawn broke on the Sabbath Day, the women sheepishly drew shawls up over their heads. Men pulled caps down over their eyes. They all scurried off home to stash their loot in under the thatch or in a hole in a stone wall before going to their house of worship to pray for forgiveness.

Bodies were left bloodied and mutilated, rolling in the waves to have their eyes pecked out by the gulls. It was one of the most shameful and shocking episodes in the local history of the Glens, and one which those involved would have preferred to forget.

Few people profited from their night's work for the peelers and excise men soon swept into the locality. One man salvaged a leather bag of gold coins, but he could not keep his mouth shut. After a few enquiries the man was found, and the treasure was seized for the crown.

There was one family – people who are well enough known locally not to be mentioned by name – they did not play any part in the gory dealings of that night. In fact, on the morning after the storm, they took it upon themselves to retrieve all the bodies they could find. They wrapped the corpses in shrouds and toiled all day with a donkey and cart to convey the dead to nearby Nappin Cemetery where they buried them in a mass, unmarked grave.

Nearly two hundred years have passed since that terrible night in 1827, and in that time those good Samaritans and their descendants have prospered. Their neighbours, on the other hand, never had any such luck. Not one of the families who bloodied their hands on that shameful night are in possession of a single acre of land. Many of them were said to have come to a bad end.

Were those who prospered favoured by Fate for their good deeds, or did they thrive by dint of riches they managed to salt away from the *Enterprise of Lynn*? It was a question often asked, for you see not all of the treasure aboard the *Enterprise of Lynn* was recovered or accounted for by the excise men.

Many years later a local fisherman, streaming close inshore for pollock, hooked something large and heavy. He pulled with all his might, thinking he was into a nice big fish. With enough to do, he got his catch to the side of the boat. As he peered over the gunwale, he could see what looked like an old leather satchel or purse encrusted with barnacles and seaweed. When he reached down into the water to take hold of it, a big hand rushed up out of the depths and made a grab for him. The bag tore open and dozens of shining, gold coins drifted down into the kelp and slowly disappeared from his sight.

The locals said he was full of imagination or drink. They said he had most likely hooked a wrasse or a wee red rock-codling in among the kelp and that a big conger eel or a seal had come up from the depths and snatched it, and that the loose scales of the devoured fish must have been what the fisherman mistook for coins glinting in the water.

Perhaps the fisherman was guilty of a little embellishment, who is to say? But there are some who think he was telling the truth, and that maybe he did see a hand in the water. Local people have often heard strange wailing and crying late at night during stormy weather. Some believe that the restless spirits of those poor sailors who perished all those years ago still jealously guard what is left of the ship's valuable cargo.

In any case, it has always been well known that the *Enterprise of Lynn* was carrying considerable riches, much of it in gold coin, very little of which was officially recovered from the wreck. For a long time after any whisper of little bits and pieces of treasure emerging always brought the peelers and excise men sniffing around.

The whole truth may never be known, but every now and then after a bout of stormy weather, the sea gave up a gold coin or a silver spoon to some lucky beachcomber or gatherer of dulse. How many and how often I cannot say, for most folk, if they had any sense, never told a living soul.

A Bird in the Hand

It was once said that falconry was the sport of kings. For generations noble men, as befitted their rank and riches, coveted the biggest, the bravest and the most beautiful peregrine falcons that could be had. The finest specimens were, and still are, to be found on the rocky crags along the wild northeast coast of Ireland.

Long, long ago when there were more kings and falcons than saints and scholars in Ireland, there was a chieftain called Cuilén Mór. He loved his wife dearly and she doted on him in return. He had four fine strong sons, but his beautiful daughter Fiona was his favourite. For her he would have moved heaven and earth.

Cuilén Mór always strived for peace with his neighbours. His people prospered. They fished and grew crops and had time to sing songs and tell stories. In turn Cuilén Mór could enjoy his favourite past-time – the ancient pursuit of falconry. He was never happier than when out hunting. Even when he was not, though, he almost always had a falcon on his gloved hand and a hound by his side.

While Cuilén Mór was away on one of his hunting trips his beloved wife died of a fever. The old chieftain was bereft. What pained him more than his own loss was to watch Fiona grieve for her mother. Cuilén Mór decided that he should take another wife so that his daughter might not feel so alone. After a hurried search for a suitable mother figure and wife for a chieftain, a match was found and a wedding was arranged.

Cuilén Mór shared a bed with his new queen to consummate their marriage, but thereafter only to sleep. He shared meals with her and discussed his daughter's upbringing, but it was plain for everyone to see that he did not love his second wife as he had the mother of his children. When Cuilén Mór was not out hunting with his birds and most faithful servant, his falconer, he was at home listening to his daughter Fiona singing and playing her harp, always with a bird in the hand.

Eventually, in a fit of jealously, the queen sought the counsel of Gráinne Dubh, Black Gráinne, as she was known. She was a wise old woman who was said to practice the dark arts.

When the queen entered the dimly lit hovel a voice said, "Ah, your majesty. I have been expecting you."

Without a flicker the queen said, "Then you know why I have come?"

"Yes. You want to do away with the two great distractions in your husband's life; his daughter and his hunting birds."

"Can you help me?"

"I can, but I must warn you that I see great danger ahead."

While the queen waited impatiently, Gráinne Dubh prepared an infusion. She handed the noble woman a vial and said, "Give this to your stepdaughter while she sleeps."

"I want her dead, but not by my hand," snapped the queen.

"Then give her this as I tell you. It will turn her into a falcon."

"A falcon!" cried the queen. "What good would that be?"

"You insult me, my queen. Do as I bid you. Fiona will fly away. When she does, tell her father that you saw a white dove flee her chamber."

"Ah. You are wise indeed Gráinne Dubh," said the queen, and she paid the old hag handsomely.

The queen did as she was instructed. When Cuilén Mór heard what had happened he fell to his knees. He knew that as a white dove Fiona would fall easy prey to a wild falcon. He gathered his four sons, and with a dozen warriors each sent them north, south, east and west saying, "Bring me the white rock dove. Do not rest or return until you have found her. And kill every falcon in this land. Leave not one alive."

His sons protested, for they knew their father revered the falcon above all creatures.

"Do as I say, and we might yet save your sister from this evil."

Lastly, and with a heavy, heavy heart, Cuilén Mór ordered his falconer to destroy every falcon perched in his mews for fear one might escape. Faithful as he was, the poor falconer could not bring himself to kill Cuilén Mór's two finest birds – a magnificent falcon and her tiercel. They were the biggest, the bravest and the most beautiful the falconer had ever seen. He cut the bells from their legs and hood-winked them, never removing their leather head coverings except by candlelight to feed them. By such means he kept them quiet and hidden in his own dwelling. Of course, Cuilén Mór's sons found no trace of any white dove, but they destroyed every falcon in the land.

With Fiona and Cuilén Mór's hunting birds gone, the queen renewed her efforts to beguile her husband. He turned his back on her. She persisted and, in his grief, he pushed her away saying, "Get out of my sight, woman."

It was the first time he had spoken roughly to her, and his words were like a cold blade through her heart. In desperation the queen returned to Gráinne Dubh.

"I warned you that I could see danger," the old woman sneered.

"If you knew what would happen why did you not stop me?"

"I can see what the future might hold, but I have no power to change it for the good."

"Can you give me back my stepdaughter?"

"That I cannot do. The spell will only be broken when true love blossoms for Fiona."

In a rage the queen drew a dagger from her sleeve and plunged it into Gráinne Dubh's heart, killing her instantly. She dropped the knife and with blood on her hands she ran to her husband crying, "I have killed the old hag who placed the enchantment on Fiona."

"What? Why did you not come to me?"

The queen wrung her hands and wailed, "I could not husband. You had turned your back on me."

Eventually Cuilén Mór said, "Did the hag speak before you killed her?"

"Only that the spell would not be broken until true love blossomed for Fiona."

"And that can never happen now," said Cuilén Mór. He fell into his wife's arms and wept bitterly. That night the queen slept in her husband's bed again.

The next day Cuilén Mór arose at dawn. He saw a falcon sitting on the bough of a dead tree not far off. Enraged, he sent for his falconer.

"Trap that bird and kill her. Do not let me see your face until you have done so."

While the falconer was setting a trap the falcon flew down and landed beside him. He caught up the bird and was about to wring its neck, but he noticed that it did not try to sink its talons into his flesh or draw blood with its powerful beak. Instinctively he felt its breastbone for signs of hunger. It was well enough fed. He looked into its eyes for traces of illness and what he saw sent a shiver down his spine. Instead of deep, dark pools it had eyes of blue – as blue as lapis stone. In former times the falconer would have shown his master, but he had been commanded to kill the bird. But instead, he hid her away. He tended it night and day. He fed it tit bits of meat from his fingers and placed silver bells on its legs.

Meanwhile, Cuilén Mór slowly began to submit to his wife's charms. She did everything she could to please him. Slowly the fog of melancholy lifted from the chieftain and his balance began to return. One day it occurred to him that he had been unjust to all but disavow his falconer. Taking his wife with him, he decided to pay a visit to the servant who had once been so loyal and valued. As he approached the falconer's dwelling, he heard the distinctive, high-pitched *kak-kak-kak* of a falcon and the sound of bells as she roused her feathers. When he saw his servant with the most magnificent falcon on his gloved hand Cuilén Mór was seized by a blind fury. He drew his sword and made to kill falcon, falconer and all.

"Wait master!" cried the falconer, and he removed the bird's hood to reveal her lapis-blue eyes. Cuilén Mór stopped in his tracks, for he had never seen the likes.

"I could not kill her, master. She was just too beautiful. In truth I have fallen in love with her."

In that instant there was a flash of light and a great puff of feathers. The falcon transformed into Fiona. She lay on the ground dressed in her tattered night gown, looking as bewildered as the falconer. Her father rushed forward to take her in his arms, but his wife screamed, "She must be a shape-shifter, husband. She is a devil. Slay her!"

"I am no devil, Father. It is I, your daughter, Fiona."

Soon the whole truth came out, as it always does in the end. The queen begged for mercy at her husband's feet, but he raised his sword to cleave her skull in two.

Fiona cried out, "No, Father. Spare her. She is your wife, for better or worse, and mother would not want her blood on our hands."

Cuilén Mór did spare his wife. After a long penance she took her place by his side once more and there she remained, for better and worse, until his death. Fiona married the gentle falconer, and they had many children together.

Cuilén Mór's two finest hunting birds – the falcon and her tiercel – were set free. They flourished. And that is why to this very day the peregrine falcons that nest on the rocky crags along the wild northeast coast of Ireland are the known to be biggest, the bravest and the most beautiful in the whole world.

The Galboly Highwaymen

In the late eighteenth century, the Glens of Antrim was not the peaceful, rural idyll we might imagine it to have been. For the peasantry living in absolute poverty, life was anything but idyllic. Being all but cut off from the rest of the country, the Glens provided the perfect hideaway for smugglers and highwaymen. They were not always the romantic characters the ballad sheets painted them to be.

These ne'er-do-wells lay about in shabeens – illegal drinking dens – where the devil made work for their idle hands. At funerals and fairs, vicious fights between rival families and gangs were commonplace. In this lawless corner of Ireland, life was hard and cheap. It was the fear of unrest and the desire to impose a degree of law and order that prompted the authorities to build what is now called the Antrim Coast Road. Back then it was known as the Grand Military Road and its sole purpose was to transport Redcoats from the garrison at Carrickfergus Castle to the heart of the Glens so that disturbances of the peace could be more easily quelled.

Then, as now, that stretch of coast between the villages of Carnlough and Waterfoot was the wildest and most remote. From the shore the terrain rises sharply to meet the high escarpment of the Antrim Plateau. Waterfalls and rock scree tumble down from sheer crags. Towering basalt pinnacles carved by wind and rain and ice make great lookout posts for falcons and ravens.

High up on a flat area about halfway along is Galboly, which means Place of the Bright Grazing. For years it has been known as the Hidden Village and has stood abandoned for decades. It was not a village at all, but a clachan: a small gathering of dwellings through which the old road ran. I say road, but it was little more than a rough track. The folk still used primitive wheelless slide carts, or slipes as they were called, dragged along by donkeys.

As enchanting as Galboly appears to us now with its breath-taking backdrop and views over Red Bay, two hundred years ago it was a den of thieves who were known as the Galboly Highwaymen. Decent folk lived there too, but in almost constant fear of the hooligans who spent their time making and drinking poitín in a shabeen attached to one of the cabins. They squabbled among themselves when they were drunk and kept the whole clachan awake at night. They plotted mischief and, occasionally, murder.

As many as sixty people scratched a living in this bleak outpost of civilisation. Cheek by jowl they were crammed into seven or eight miserably small, stone-built, thatched-roofed cabins. They are only skeletons of habitation now, but the bare timbers and windowless wallsteads are not the only skeletons left behind by their former tenants.

There was once a widow woman by the name of Fairley who lived deep in the Glens of Antrim. She was up in years and very lonely since her family were all away. She lived by the goodwill of the parish and what little food she could gather from along the seashore.

One day she received a letter from her son Jasper in America, but she had to take it to the priest in Waterfoot to have it read for her. It said that Jasper was coming home to Ireland and that she need never worry more, for now her son was a rich man.

Well, the old widow Fairley lived a stone's throw from Galboly in the next townland of Falavee. She was far enough away to not be bothered by the late-night shenanigans of her nearest neighbours, but close enough to have her business discussed by them. When she received the good news from her son, even though the priest warned her against it, she could not help but tell all and sundry what was contained in the letter. This caused her and her son to become of interest to the Galboly Highwaymen.

For months the old woman carried the letter about with her. She stared at it as if she understood every word and waved it in the faces of her poor, illiterate neighbours as proof of her good fortune. She took to going down to the pier at Falavee every day to wait for the arrival of a tall ship from which her son would come swaggering down the gang plank. Falavee was the place where her son had joined a passing schooner many years earlier. It must have seemed reasonable to her that he would make his return at the same place.

The weeks became months, and the months became years. The letter became tattered and torn and bit by bit blew away in the wind. Faithfully the widow kept her daily vigil. Ships appeared on the horizon, and she would get her hopes up only to have them dashed again when the ship sailed on. Ships did come into Red Bay and on occasion tied up at Falavee Pier. She would question every sailor who came ashore, but none had ever heard of her son Jasper.

As time passed, she became more and more frantic. Her hair grew wild and her clothes fell into rags. Driven to distraction, she eventually passed away not knowing if her son was alive or dead. But there were those in Galboly who knew exactly what had become of Jasper Fairley. Whether it was by way of drunken boastfulness, idle gossip or guilty confession, the truth leached out of that barren, rocky place.

Jasper Fairley had returned to Ireland. He disembarked a ship at Belfast and made his way by coach and horses as far as Larne and from there to Glenarm and Carnlough. From

Garron Point he walked the last few miles toward his family home just beyond Galboly at Falavee. He thought he would meet some old acquaintances the nearer he came to home, but with his cocked hat, topcoat and high leather boots, his mother might not have recognised him, so fine a gentleman had he become. Nevertheless, news of his arrival travelled faster than he did.

As he approached Galboly and the old familiar track that climbed up the steep hillside, Jasper became more and more uneasy. He kept a ready hand to the butt of the pistol he carried inside his coat. In the moonlight every passing cloud cast a shadow. Every stir of the wind through the trees kept him on edge. When an animal scurried across the track in front of him, Jasper drew his pistol.

"Who's there?" he cried, but there was no answer.

As he rounded a bend, pistol still in his hand, a figure stepped from the shadow of a big rock.

"Is that Jasper? Jasper Fairley?" the man said. "It is yourself, by God. Strike me down man, I hardly knew ye."

Jasper recognised the voice. He had known it since childhood when he ran the countryside barefoot with all the other young lads of the parish.

"We hear you've made a fortune of money in America, Jasper."

"We?" said Jasper, suspiciously.

"Me and the Galboly boys."

Just then another man appeared from the other side of the track. "You wouldn't have any of that money on you Jasper, would ye?"

Jasper raised the pistol at him. "I warn you, I will use this if I have to."

"Ah, c'mon Jasper. We're only having a carryin' on," the first man said. "Tell us where you keep your money – under that big, cocked hat?"

In answer to him, Jasper swung the pistol around and drew a bead on his forehead, but the second man tipped Jasper's hat off with the shillelagh he was carrying. There was a loud report from the pistol as its lead ball was fired harmlessly into the dark. At the same time an unseen man brought a stone mace down on Jasper and broke his skull with a sickening crack.

For their night's work the Galboly Highwaymen gained a handful of silver, a pocket watch and their victim's expensive clothing. If they had been able to read, they would have discovered that Jasper Fairley carried the deed that staked his claim to one of the richest goldmines in California. Along with it was a receipt for a twenty thousand dollars deposited with the Union Bank in Boston, and two tickets for passage to New York out of Liverpool. These papers were burned in the fire of their shabeen.

It is said that all those Galboly Highwaymen came to a bad end. One by one they either drunk themselves to death or were killed in drunken brawls, and at least one went to the gallows. Many years later, surface men quarrying limestone to maintain the coast road uncovered a skeleton in a rocky crevice near Galboly. The skull had been stove in. Those with the longest memories said it was the remains of Jasper Fairley, murdered and entombed by the Galboly Highwaymen.

Local scholars have put forward different ideas as to why Galboly fell to wreck and ruin and was eventually abandoned in the 1960s. Some said it was the inevitable consequence of being bypassed by the new coast road over a hundred years earlier. Others said it was just the changing times and the migration of people from the countryside to the towns.

But some folk think it was the ghost of Jasper Fairley unhurriedly exacting revenge on his killers and those who turned a blind eye to their crimes. If that seems too fanciful for you, let me remind you of a wise old saying: *The wheels of justice turn slowly but grind exceedingly fine.*

The Wise Woman of Ballyeamon

Once upon a time people believed that a stone-age axe washed out of a riverbank was the remains of a thunder bolt come to earth. It was said the best time to find one was nine days after the storm that delivered it. These stones, fallen from the sky, were charged with great power. Likewise, prehistoric flint arrow points turned up by farmers' ploughs and known as "elf-shot" were also imbued with magic. They were said to be the remains of darts fired by mischievous faerie folk, intent on harming beasts of the field and some poor farmer's prospects.

In the wrong hands, untold havoc could be wreaked by these powerful objects, but in the hands of a good-hearted wise woman, their potential for healing was limitless. It's not so many years ago that people the length and breadth of the country relied on the knowledge, the skill and the good judgement of these wise women or hen-wives, as they were sometimes called. Their wisdom was handed down through the generations from mother to daughter. They brought babies into the world that might otherwise have died in their mother's womb, and they prepared the bodies of the dead for their journey into the next realm. They were often consulted on affairs of the heart and delicate matters of intimacy. Wise women were revered, sometimes feared and occasionally maligned as witches.

This very thing happened to a poor woman from Glenballyeamon who lived in the shadow of Tievebulliagh mountain. How she fell so low in the estimation of her neighbour folk after so many years of being held in the highest regard came down to one man – the newly appointed parish priest. He had blown in from Belfast and had no time whatsoever for what he called "satanic rituals".

"They must cease forthwith," he said from the alter. "Put your faith in the Lord Jesus Christ. Light a candle and make a small offering to God. (And for other temporal matters, my good friend the doctor will be only too glad to provide his services.) But these dark practices, carried out in the middle of the night by candlelight, must stop!"

Even though deep down in their heart of hearts the folk still believed in the power of the ancient remedies, they were swayed against this wise woman. Overnight she became an outcast. Far too easily they disremembered her charm for warts: the old copper coin placed over the growth, the insistence of no payment and no spoken word of thanks. They forgot about her ointments and poultices for everything from the toothache to a boil. And they forgot about her infusions of wild herbs and tonics for everything from constipation to infertility.

The rare and treasured polished stone thunder bolt, handed down from mother to daughter and passed around the belly to ease menstrual pain or the agony of labour contractions in women, and animals, was suddenly of no value. The people believed the priest when he told them it was just a piece of black flint fashioned into a tool by the earliest people of Ireland.

The elf-shots, boiled in goat's milk with carefully chosen herbs, strained and taken to stimulate the flow of breast milk, were scorned. The priest said they were only the tips of arrows lost by human hunters long, long ago.

"These things," he said, "interesting as they might be to antiquarians, have no more power than a pebble found on the beach. Do not be duped by this evil black magic!"

And so, the people put all their faith in the Lord Jesus Christ. They lit candles and they made offerings of ha'pennies they could little-afford, but of course their purse could not stretch to a doctor's fee. Warts went uncured. Toothaches tormented people and kept them awake. There was no one to summon late at night when there were difficulties with a cow in calf or a mare in foal. Children were taken by fevers, and babies were born still.

With little understanding and nowhere else to turn, the people began to blame the wise woman of Glenballyeamon for all their ills and misfortune. They said she was in cahoots with the other crowd – the Faerie Folk – and that she even consorted with the Oul Nick himself. No one seemed to notice that for all her great powers and connections with the underworld she was just as poor as they were. She had nothing to show for all her evil endeavours. And yet they persecuted her. She was openly mocked and condemned as a witch.

"You must repent and mend your ungodly ways," the priest told her.

"Go to hell," was her answer.

Late one night the thatch of her cottage was set alight. As the roof timbers crackled in the blaze, she and her family fled into the darkness and never returned to that townland. Some said they emigrated to England or America. Some said they saw her at the Lammas Fair in Ballycastle selling trinkets and cough bottles. Those who knew her best or who were related to her never spoke of her again for fear they might bring trouble to their own doors. The story of the Glenballyeamon wise woman accused of witchcraft and burned out of her home faded and was forgotten.

Time passed and three or maybe four generations later a young woman returned to visit the wallstead of her ancestor's home. The story of the wise woman had survived in her family by being passed down from mother to daughter until the present day. The young woman could only imagine her great, great grandmother preparing ancient remedies in the kitchen of her tiny cottage, long since tumbled down. She walked among the stones trying to summon the spirit of her forebear.

A byre where the animals were once kept remained. It had not been burned. The thatch had long ago fallen in and been replaced by a corrugated iron roof – now rusted red. But the building was, more or less, as it always had been. The young woman entered without fear as swallows swooped out past her to escape into the blue daylight.

She felt in between the rafters along the tops of the thick stone walls where it had been whispered the tools of her ancestor's trade were kept – it being far too dangerous to keep such powerful medicinal things in the dwelling house. Decades of mortar dust, decayed thatch and spider's webs did not deter her.

Eventually she found a ragged parcel of calico tied by a piece of twine. She delicately unwrapped it and found a big copper cartwheel penny – the old charm for warts! There was a black polished stone-age axe, believed by her ancestor to be a thunder bolt fallen from the sky. There were a handful of flint arrowheads said to be the faerie darts. The young woman was breathless and her heart beat like a bodhran in her breast. For her the magic of these things was not diminished by the harsh light of understanding. The pride and deep connection to her grandmother of all those years ago burned warmly inside.

The young woman took the ancient artefacts home. She keeps them with all her most treasured possessions. They are in a box by her bed, together with beautiful heartfelt letters written by grateful mothers, thanking her for the safe and skilful delivery of their babies. These mean more to her than the certificates on the wall that tell the modern world she is a midwife.

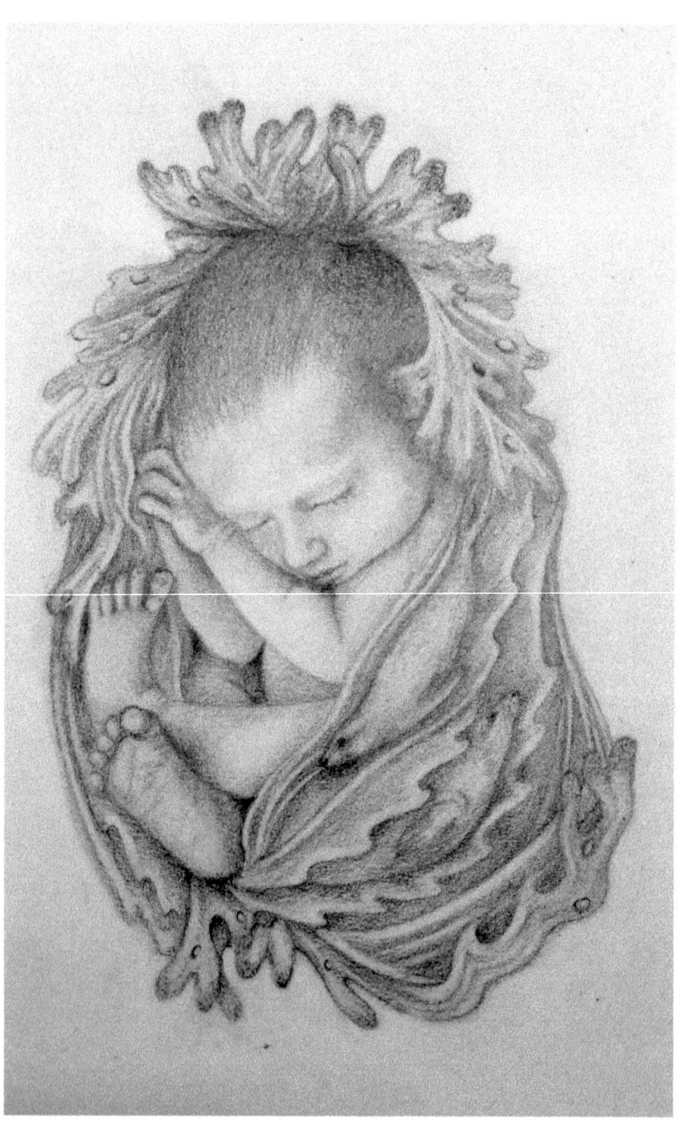

John o the Sea

There was once a fisherman called Daniel who lived with his wife Martha down by the shore near the village of Waterfoot. Daniel sold some fish and Martha salted the rest to see them through leaner times. Martha fertilized her potato rigs with seaweed and she gathered driftwood for burning. Like most of their neighbours they lived a hand to mouth existence.

Now in those days seal skin was in great demand, especially to make waterproof garments for sailors and pouches to keep their tobacco dry. Daniel could have improved their lot by hunting seals and selling their pelts, but he was a deeply superstitious man. He always said, "No man can tell the difference between a seal and a one of the seal people. They are the reincarnation of drowned souls. To harm one of them, even by mistake, would bring terrible misfortune." Even when a dead seal washed up near their wee cabin, Daniel dug a grave in the sand and buried it, just in case it was one of the seal people.

All things considered, Daniel and Martha seemed content enough, but there was always an emptiness in their home. As the years went by, they slowly resigned themselves to the reality that there never would be the sound of a gurgling baby on a rug by the fire or the laughter of a child at play. A cradle Daniel had made years before was quietly moved out to the shed. The wee bonnets and gowns Martha had knitted with great hope were ripped out and turned into socks for her husband.

One night a knock came to their door. Daniel answered it, and silhouetted against the moonlight was a gentleman dressed in black from head to toe.

"Come in and welcome," said Daniel, but the man refused.

"I have come to beg for your help," he said, and from under his cloak he handed Daniel a bundle. "Take good care of him. He is precious to me."

Daniel looked down. It was a baby wrapped up in seaweed. When he lifted his eyes again the stranger was gone into the night. Daniel put the door back on the latch and brought the child into Martha. She stripped away the swaddling, such as it was, to reveal the most beautiful baby boy you could imagine. His skin was as pure as freshly fallen snow and as soft as a rose petal, and on his wee head was a velvety down of black hair.

Well Daniel and Martha had many questions they would have liked answers to, but the whys and the wherefores would all have to wait. They had a child to look after, and the first thing they needed was milk. A kettle was boiled on the fire. Bread was soaked and strained through a muslin cloth. Goats milk and cream were added, and the child took it as if it was straight from his mother's breast. The cradle was brought back in from the shed and dusted down. The child was tucked up in a blanket and slept – well, just like a baby.

"What do we call him?" Daniel said.

After some thought Martha announced, "We'll call him after John the disciple. May he live a happy life and die of old age." And with a sprinkling of holy water, she baptised the child, "In the name of the Father, the Son and the Holy Spirit. Amen."

Well, the neighbours were told that the child was a foundling left on their doorstep, which wasn't so uncommon in those days. From then on, he became known to locals as John o the Sea. Before Martha and Daniel knew it, he was crawling about on all fours, and the next thing he was walking. His hair grew into a mane of curls the colour of wet coals and his big eyes were dark and intelligent. He was the most handsome, loveable child and he was as healthy as a trout too. No matter what chills or fevers came about – and there were plenty in those days – he was never taken ill.

John o the Sea's young life was free of all care. His adoptive parents never explained the queer way in which he had come to them, and he didn't know to ask. He only ever addressed them by their name Christian names. They had never insisted on anything else. Daniel taught John how to knit nets and make repairs to the boat. He showed him all his best fishing marks, and John found a few of his own that were better. Daniel hoped that one day John would take over from him, but every mother wants better for their child, and Martha was no different.

"We'll have to get John educated," she said one day.

"But where would we get the money?" asked Daniel.

Martha had it all worked out. "You could hunt for seals and sell their pelts," she ventured.

"No man can tell the difference between a seal and one of the seal people. They are the reincarnation of drowned souls. If I harmed one of them, even by mistake, it would bring terrible misfortune."

Martha dismissed her husband's foolish superstitions, and she rattled on and on. Eventually, to pacify her, Daniel agreed. "On your head be it," he said.

He fashioned a harpoon out of a fire iron and lashed it to a hazel pole. When young John realised what his father was doing, he was furious and refused to help. But when he saw Daniel putting to sea on his own, he felt guilty and went along.

The seals had no fear of Daniel's boat. He had often tossed them a mackerel when the fishing was good, so they came close.

When Daniel raised his harpoon to strike, John often stopped him and said, "No, not this one," or "No, not that one." John was so adamant and serious that Daniel always let him have his way. Daniel harpooned many seals, but John flatly refused to help with the gory work of skinning. The pelts were sold, and soon Daniel began to see his small savings grow.

Time passed and as John approached manhood he became a fine big strapping lump of a youth – over six foot tall and well made. All the young maids of the village were keen to catch his eye, but he seemed to be blind to their attentions. Like a lot of young lads, he soon became independent, and very private in his habits. He would often go out at night and not return till the morning. He always said he had been fishing, and sometimes he would have a cod or a few mackerel for the table.

Martha always tongued, "That boy is going to be drowned out there on his own some night, and all for the sake of a few miserable oul fish." She urged her husband to greater pains to earn the money for sending John off to be educated.

No matter when Daniel went to hunt the seals John was always on hand to help, in his own peculiar way. But Daniel was getting more and more confident. One morning he rose early, and without calling John from his bed he went out by himself. Not far off the shore he saw a large bull seal lying on the top of the water, distracted by a cow nearby. Daniel had never tackled a bull before, always the smaller females. But this big bull's pelt would fetch three times the money. How much more difficult could it be?

Daniel raised his harpoon and struck down with all his might into the animal's back. It let out a merciful cry and dived beneath the waves. The rope ran out through Daniel's hands and burned them to the bone. When the rope came up hard against the stern post it nearly pulled the boat under the water, and Daniel had to cut it to save himself. With nothing but a pair of sore hands to show for his efforts, Daniel slowly rowed for home.

When he walked in his wife enquired about John.

"How should I know? He must be lying in his bed," said Daniel.

"His bed hasn't even been slept in," Martha answered.

All day they waited, and no word of John. A heavy burden of despair began to descend on them. Martha paced the floor pulling her hair out and wringing her hands.

After midnight there came a loud knocking at the door. Daniel rushed to answer it. There stood the same gentleman dressed in black who had brought John almost twenty years earlier. He bid Daniel to follow him with great speed. There on the sand below the cabin lay John, naked and senseless. He was all but dead. Daniel oxtercogged him indoors. A deep wound just below his left shoulder-blade gaped wide open. Martha staunched the bleeding, and with herbs and clean linen dressed it every few hours.

For a week John walked a tightrope between life and death. Every night the gentleman dressed in black came to ask after him. Martha lit candles and prayed. Daniel lamented, "It's all my fault. No man can tell the difference between a seal and a selkie. I have brought terrible misfortune down on us."

On the eighth morning John opened his eyes, and when he saw Daniel and Martha he smiled. "Dearest Father and Mother, you have saved my life."

It was the first time John had ever named them in a sonly way.

"I almost took your life, John. It was the strange gentleman who saved you," said Daniel. "Tell us, son, who is he?"

Eventually John explained, "He is one of the seal people, the one who sired me. My birth mother died as she gave life to me. It was her remains you buried. Rather than leave me for dead, my rearing was entrusted to you."

The tears were tripping Martha and through them she said, "We have loved you, John, as if you were our very own flesh and blood. Return to your own kind, son, with our blessing."

John took her hand and said, "I had to know from where I came Mother, but I wish to spend the rest of my days here, if you and Father still want me."

Well, Martha wept all the more, but her tears of sadness became floods of joy.

And that is the story of John o the Sea, the newborn seal child who was adopted by a fisherman and his wife long ago. Martha gave over her idea to send John away to be educated. He followed in the footsteps of his adoptive father and, just in case you're wondering, Daniel never hunted seals again!

Over time John o the Sea became John O'Shea. He married a land woman and together they had children of their own and the O'Shea name was passed on. Even to this day male descendants of the O'Sheas are often born with little webs of skin between their toes, and the name is forever associated with the seal folk.

When John was a very old man people used to ask him to what he attributed his long and healthy life. He always told them, "A diet of fish, a swim in the sea every day and the love of good, honest parents."

The House Maid

Many long years ago in the Glens of Antrim, when the call of the corncrake still kept folk awake at night and sailing ships jostled for a safe berth in river mouths and harbours up and down the coast, Noleen McAuley lived on a farm near the foot of Glenballyeamon. She was only sixteen years old when she walked the three or so miles to Cushendun to enter service as a house maid. Her new employers, a family by the name of McSparron, ran a hotel and other businesses, so they were well enough heeled. Noleen started work for them that October.

She wasn't there long until she caught the eye of the youngest son of the family. His name was Matthew McSparron. Everyone except his parents called him Mattie, and Noleen had an eye for him too. Being a little naïve as to the ways of the world, Noleen was flattered that Mattie showed interest in one as lowly and as young as she, for he was a good five years older and there were much finer young ladies in the village and roundabout.

More than once they met on the back stairs or in the parlour and shared a few moments of warmth. Before long Noleen could hardly concentrate on her work, but when Mattie asked her to meet him down by the caves one warm summer night, she was beside herself with excitement.

All through the autumn and winter the young couple courted in secret, and Mattie turned Nora's wee head with wonderful tales of travel to big cities. He promised to take her to see the hustle and bustle of Dublin and Glasgow and even London!

"Wait till you see, Noleen," he would say, "you won't believe your eyes."

Truth was Mattie had never been further than Belfast himself, but Noleen didn't know that, and she was swept off her feet by all his big talk and promises.

"When can we go?" she used to ask.

"Just as soon as we're married, my love," Mattie would answer.

Time passed and by the spring Nora was noticing some strange things happening to her. She was sick as a dog every morning, but it was one of the older girls who told her what it was.

"Somebody's filled your wee belly, haven't they?"

"What?" said Noleen.

"You're up the pole, Nora! You've a cake in the oven. You're having a wean!"

Nora was mortified. She didn't know whether to run away or throw herself into the tide.

"It'll be alright," said Mattie. "Dry your eyes and don't worry your head about a thing."

"I love you, Mattie," she said. "When can we be married?"

"As soon as I can arrange everything, my love," he said. His words soothed and reassured Noleen, and eventually she stopped weeping. "But you can't stay here. Now that we're to be married it would be bad luck. You'll have to go home and get ready for the wedding. I will send word when everything is prepared."

Well, Noleen went home chirping like a bird. Her mother was disbelieving at first, but Noleen's happiness was catching, and soon everyone in the McAuley household was as excited as she was. Her mother set to work. From her own wedding gown she made Noleen the prettiest dress and a veil.

"It's beautiful, Ma," said Noleen, and tears rose to her eyes again.

As the spring wore on into April there was still no word from Mattie. Eventually rumours came that he had disappeared – gone to Scotland the people said.

"It can't be right," said Noleen. "Mattie promised me faithfully."

But seemingly it was true. Mattie had left Noleen in the lurch, and now it was as plain as day to everyone that she had a baby growing inside her. Noleen's father never spoke a word for a week. Her brothers cursed and swore they would kill Mattie McSparron, even if it meant the gallows for them, and her mother wept.

By May Eve Noleen was out of her mind with grief and worry. She rose from her bed, put on her wedding gown and went out walking through the fields. It was long past the hour when a young woman should be out alone, but she needed to be away from her family and her fears. Someone said they saw her walking down towards the village of Cushendall all dressed in white, but that was the last anyone heard of Noleen McAuley. Just like that she vanished.

Of course, a search was made. High up and low down the neighbours hunted, but no trace of Noleen could be found. Eventually her family had to accept that she had probably thrown herself into the river or the tide, heartbroken as she was. It was an all-too-common story of false love and the terrible shame of a child that would be born out of wedlock. And now it had all ended in tragedy.

The time passed slowly, and though her family and friends scoured the beaches for Noleen's body and waited for word, none came. Then one day it was whispered that Mattie McSparron had returned from his exile in Scotland. He had been seen at the Lammas Fair in Ballycastle. Some even said he had never even been away. Tongues wagged, and soon a rumour was going around that maybe Mattie McSparron had something to do with his young lover's disappearance. The folk began to whisper that the likes of Mattie McSparron could get away with murder, and that folk like him were never held to account for any wrongdoing.

Noleen's brothers kept their ears to the ground, and eventually they heard that Mattie was drinking in a Shabeen – and illegal drinking den – away up in Glendun. It didn't take long to track him down and discover his nocturnal habits. As he staggered along the road by the light of the moon one evening, he was set upon. A sack was pulled over his head. His wrists were bound behind his back and a hempen noose placed around his neck.

"You are going to swing for your crimes, you bastard," one of Noleen's brothers said.

"What crimes?" cried Mattie, emboldened by whiskey.

"You murdered our sister," another cried, "and you're going to pay for it."

"A rogue and a wretch I may be, but I murdered no one. I loved Noleen."

"Loved her? Well, you had a quare way of showing it. Now you can go and join her!"

The loose end of the rope was thrown over the bough of an oak tree. Noleen's brothers began to haul up the slack.

As the noose tightened around Mattie's neck he sobbed uncontrollably. "Before you put me out of my misery know this: I loved your sister. In my pocket is a letter and a wedding ring. I beg you, please, give it to your mother. My intentions were honourable, if far too late."

Well, the brothers looked at each other. The rope was slackened, and Mattie's body slumped to the ground. They searched his pockets and there they found a letter dated the day Noleen went missing. The words were smudged where teardrops had fallen on the ink, and it had been read many times. "Dearest Noleen, please forgive my delay," it read. "Fear not, I am coming for you my love …" In the envelope was a gold wedding band.

"He's trying to save his neck. String him up I say," said one brother.

But John, the eldest, overruled him. "Look at him, he's a miserable cur. Hanging is too good for him. We'll let him live."

And although Noleen's brothers still cursed Mattie McSparron for being the source of all their family's grief and woe, they could not bring themselves to murder him. They unbound him, left him whimpering where he lay and took the letter home to their mother. It gave her little comfort but at least the gossipmongers might be silenced. She said it eased her pain a bit to think her daughter might not have been so foolish as to be completely duped.

Time passed, as it always does, and the family bore their loss with great dignity and resolve. The following May Eve Noleen's eldest brother was returning from a late-night tryst with a local farmer's daughter. It was near midnight when he came tripping up the road, his feet as light as feathers from the excitement of his first kiss. Not a mile away from his home he heard a woman's voice calling his name in an urgent whisper.

"John, John."

He scanned the darkness and suddenly, through the hazel and thorns he caught a faint glimmer of white. As he did so, his ears were filled with distant music and chattering and laughter. It was a procession of faerie folk. In the middle of them was his sister Noleen. She beckoned him to follow her. The faeries seemed to take no notice of his presence as he jostled and jinked to get closer to his sister.

"Noleen, is it really you or am I dreaming?" he asked.

Noleen smiled but never answered. She made eyes at her brother to stay quiet and close.

Eventually the faeries came to a place called Tiveragh – the faerie hill – which seemed to open to allow them entry. Noleen shook her head imperceptibly to make her brother understand he should be very careful.

"Help me," she mouthed silently just before she disappeared into the ground.

John was left outside as the last of the faerie folk trooped into the hill. The last one stopped and turned to John, and as if noticing him for the first time said very charmingly, "Come in John, and you're welcome."

In an instant John had to decide whether to fight for his sister or flee for his life. He bent down to untie his laces. Taking off his big iron-shod hob-nailed boots he left them at the threshold as he entered the hill.

Inside was a great chamber the size of a church and lit by flaming torches and candles of bee's wax. There were great trestle tables ladened with all kinds of breads and meat, and bottles and jugs of whiskey and mead. There were pipers and harpists and fiddlers and drummers all tearing away at jigs and reels the like of which John had never heard. He couldn't keep his feet still, so good was the music. Every time he turned around he was offered a plateful of food or a tumblerful of drink. Each time, he looked up to see his sister making eyes that warned him not to partake. Eventually, he made his way close to where Noleen was seated at the top table. As he leaned down, she was able to whisper into his ear.

"Take nothing from them or you might never be able to return to the human world."

John looked at his sister. She was dressed in her wedding gown and was just as he remembered, though she was no longer with child. As his eyes flitted over her slender waist Noleen answered his enquiry.

"I gave birth here and can have my freedom anytime, but I cannot leave my daughter. It was only her they wanted."

"Where is she?" whispered John anxiously.

"She is brought to me every day to nurse, but is taken away again, to where I do not know. Help us, please, John."

Their brief conversation was interrupted by an ancient faerie man who was evidently of some importance, for all the other faeries seemed to defer to him. "Come and sit with me, John," he said, "and enjoy our hospitality, for it is freely given."

John sat down beside the wee man, and again he was offered platters of the finest food and tumblers of drink. Although his stomach was rumbling and groaning, John politely refused any and all such offerings.

"Have you come for your sister?" asked the wee man abruptly.

"I have," said John, just as short.

"Take her with ye then, she's free to go anytime. She'd have been welcome to stay but she's too full of grief and woe for our liking."

"Maybe if you'd let her have her daughter she'd grieve less."

"Ah, no," said the wee man, "I fear she was full of sadness long before she came to us."

"Came to ye? I'm sure she didn't come here of her own free will."

"You did, John," said the wee man mockingly. "But anyway, Nora is free to go now. Take her home, with my blessing."

"In the name of all that's good, would you not let her see her child one more time?"

The wee faerie man looked at John as if studying his face for some clue of his intent.

"In the name of all that *is* good, I will," he said, and snapped his fingers.

The next thing, a child wrapped in a swaddling was brought out by a wee faerie woman and Noleen was summoned. She was asked if she wanted to nurse the child one more time. Noleen looked at John, and he nodded and smiled at her. While all this was going on John lifted a bottle of the whiskey as if he was about to drown the wean's head, for of course he had never had the chance to celebrate the birth of his niece. But instead of putting the bottle to his lips, he smashed it off the wall at the nearest flaming torch.

There was great blue flash of burning spirit which frightened the living daylights out of all the wee folk. They cowered, and the music stopped dead. John seized another bottle and another and did the very same with those. In the confusion he took hold of his sister with the child in her arms and kept the faeries at bay by brandishing his pocketknife like a sabre. The blade was only about four or five inches long, but of course it was forged of iron, and that metal is the one thing the faeries fear the most in the world.

John smashed eight, nine, ten bottles of whiskey and wreaked havoc as they hurriedly backed out of that faerie mound. The portal to the human world was still ajar, for John had the wit and good foresight to keep it open with his big ignorant iron-shod hob-nailed boots, which no faerie would ever have dared lay a hand to. As soon as they were outside the faerie mound in the cool night air, John gave his sister a shove in the direction of home.

"Take that wean and run for your life, Noleen. Don't stop or look behind ye."

And that's what she did. She took to her heels, screaming and screeching all the way. Before she got to her front door her father and young brothers were standing out in the cassie with fire irons and shillelaghs in hand.

"John's down at Tiveragh – he needs help!" Noleen gasped before she collapsed.

Well, the sudden reappearance of Noleen in her wedding dress bearing a child in her arms was disconcerting and confusing in the extreme. But her mention of the faerie hill was all her father and brothers needed to straightaway make sense of the situation. They ran down the lane calling John's name, and when they got there saw he was surrounded by wee wicked, snarling faerie folk, who looked as if they would have torn him to pieces if respite had not arrived in the nick of time. Confronted by John's enraged fireiron-wielding father and brothers, the faerie folk vanished, and in an instant the night became as silent as the grave.

It took the rest of the dark hours for Noleen to tell how she had been taken by the faeries and all that had happened to her in the year she had been away. Every now and then she would look at her baby daughter nuzzled in at her breast and just burst into tears, but they were tears of joy and relief.

As dawn broke, John and his younger brothers sheepishly told how they had meant to hang Mattie McSparron but, in the end, had spared his miserable life. Their mother took out the letter with the gold wedding band. Noleen read it several times over before she put it aside.

"If he wants me and his daughter, he will come to us," she said. "If not, he can run on."

It didn't take long for word to spread round the villages and clachans of the Glens of Antrim about Noleen McAuley's miraculous return. Of course, some said she had been sent away to relatives to have the wean and that the faeries had nothing at all to do with it. Most were not so sure.

When Mattie heard the news, he left off his drinking, tidied himself up and, just as soon as he could, came to beg Noleen's forgiveness and ask for her hand in marriage all over. He vowed never to leave her side again. She accepted his proposal. They were duly married, though not without some resistance from family members on both sides.

Whether they lived happily ever after or not I couldn't tell you, but they say that Mattie McSparron made good on all his promises, and that he and Noleen travelled together as far as Dublin and Glasgow and London, aye, and even Paris and New York.

The Salmon Man

Not so many years ago, there was a farmer called Randal. The Glendun River ran down through his land to the sea. His animals drank from the river and cooled themselves in the summer. When Randal was a boy he had often tickled trout along its banks, catching them with nothing more than his bare hands. As an older man he cared for the river, some people said, even more than he did his own farm. He trained trees to grow over the pools, to shade the salmon where they lay. And he fenced off the banks along the gravel redds where they spawned to keep the cattle from disturbing them.

He fished for the salmon with a greenheart rod and jewel-like flies he tied himself from the gaudy feathers of the pheasant and the jay. He purposefully blunted his hooks so not to harm the fish, and in all his years he never killed a single one. He only marvelled at their beauty and returned them to the water to go on their way, often helping them over a rapid. Some people said they had heard him talking to the fish. They said he was touched, and behind his back they called him the Mad Salmon Man.

Randal was a widower. He had a family of four daughters, all grown up and away, and one son called Bradán, the Irish name for salmon. It was always understood that Bradán would one day take over the farm. He shared his father's love of the river and the salmon. As a boy, his father had taught him how to fish in the same gentle way. As they sat by the river his father told him the wonderful story of how the young salmon went on a great adventure into the wild Atlantic Ocean, how they faced all kinds of dangers and enemies before returning to their native glen and the river where they were spawned.

Bradán grew into a fine young man. Everyone said he was the spit of his father. He was clever and handsome and full of ideas. He told his father he wanted to make the best of what mother nature and providence had granted them. "We could bring fine gentleman here to fish," he said. "Rich anglers would pay good money to catch our salmon in such beautiful surroundings."

"They are not our salmon son," his father said. "They're wild and free. We would have to cut trees down to make way for these gentlemen. They would kill every fish they caught. We must watch over the river, not profit from it."

It was the same when Bradán wanted to make changes on the farm – dig a drain through the meadow or make a ford across the river. His father was always opposed.

"New kings make new laws," he said. "Your time will come, but by then you will be older and wiser."

Bradán respected his father, but still and all he felt frustrated. He wanted to make his mark on the world. He began to look outwards to satisfy his ambitious. Young men from the Glens who did not inherit their father's farm or could not make a decent living from it often inclined towards the sea. Bradán watched the tall ships come into Cushendun Bay and sail away again. A seed of an idea began to germinate in his mind.

One day he announced, "Father, I am going away to see the world and make my fortune."

Randal fell into a deep melancholy. He knew that once his son got the taste for adventure, or found a wife in some foreign land, he might never return. As always, Randal went to the river to think about things. He took his fishing rod and his net, but this day he just sat by a pool and smoked his pipe in quiet contemplation. He watched the dippers bobbing up and down beneath the fast-flowing streams and a kingfisher diving from its perch to take the minnows in the shallows. He saw a family of otters at play and a heron standing motionless on one leg. It came to him that every living thing must follow its own nature. Although the sadness weighed on him heavily, Randal knew then that his son must find his own way to become a man.

And then suddenly a huge salmon's back broke the water, black and shining. It happened again, so Randal half-heartedly cast his fly. The fish snatched it first time. Without much of a fight, he brought it to the side and caught it up in his net. As he lay it on the grassy bank to remove the hook, the fish spoke!

"Do you remember me, Randal?"

Randal rocked back on his heels. "Salar? It cannot be?" he said.

"I assure you it can, and it is," said the fish. "I am King of the Salmon now. You have been a friend to us always. Now you are in need, let me be a friend to you."

"But Salar, how?"

"Bring your son here to me. I will show him something of the world and, if he survives, I will return him to his native glen, and he can follow this river home."

"But what if he were to be eaten or killed?"

"There are many dangers in this world, Randal, but I give you my word I will do all in my power, which is considerable, to return him to you."

Well, Randal went away home with his mind in turmoil, and the weeks passed. The night before young Bradán was due to depart, Randal asked his son to take one last walk down to the river with him. Bradán was busy packing his gear, but his father was so forlorn he could not refuse.

When they came to the pool where Randal had caught Salar, he said, "Please, sit down a minute, son."

"Yes, Father," Bradán said.

The conversation was awkward. Randal began to feel guilty and foolish. Then suddenly he saw the back of a salmon break the water. Just then there was a great flash of light, and flipping and flapping on the bank where Bradán had been sitting was a little silver salmon smolt, the length of a man's hand. Randal guided it into the Brown River, and it took off in a fizz of bubbles. It skipped and splashed on the surface of the pool before disappearing downstream.

Salar's head appeared above the water. "Be here next autumn," he said. "You will need to catch your son to have him back."

Randal had a year to wait, but when the salmon returned the following autumn he lived up to his reputation as the Mad Salmon Man. He fished the Glendun River morning, noon and night. He caught dozens of fish and released every single one. He went out in the dark with a lantern to scare off poachers and otters. He spent every waking hour, and the hours he should have been sleeping, on the river. He watched the salmon at rest in their lies. He watched them leap up and over the falls and spawn in their redds, but there was no sign of Bradán.

Autumn turned to winter. Winter turned to spring, spring to summer, and summer to autumn once more. It was the same again. Dozens of fish caught, and no sight or sign of his son. Randal began to curse his stupidity.

"Salar has tricked me. He's a cold-blooded fish. What would he know of a young man's needs or a father's love?"

The following autumn Randal dragged himself to the river. He could not give up while there was glimmer of hope or an ounce of strength left in him. He caught dozens more fish and released them all. And then on the very last day of the season, he was watching the salmon gather in the shallows. A hen fish turned on her side, and with a few swishes of her tail she hollowed out a nest. A large copper-coloured cock fish rushed in and danced in ecstasy alongside her. As she released hundreds of tiny glowing pink eggs, he covered them with his milk, and together they buried them in the gravel.

Randal cast his line and the spent fish rose to the fly. He took it delicately in his mouth. Randal brought it gently to the side and eased it into his net. He lifted it clear of the water, and the moment he laid it on the grassy bank there was a flash of light. Bradán lay there, coughing and gasping for breath, his skin pale and his lips blue. Randal clapped his back and rubbed his limbs. He took off his coat and draped it over his son, and he laughed and laughed and cried tears of joy.

That night Bradán sat with his feet almost in the fire trying to heat them. He told his father how he had crossed the ocean with Salar, been hunted by seals and dolphins, seen great whales and giant sea monsters in battle, escaped the jaws of a shark and the nets of fishermen. He told about swimming under great blue icebergs the size of mountains in the land of the midnight sun, and sang strange sea shanties he had learned from wise old seabirds and ancient turtles.

"But when the impulse to return came upon me," he said, "I never stopped for food or rest until I reached Cushendun Bay!"

In the weeks and months and years that followed, Bradán rarely spoke of his adventures, although he was often heard singing his strange songs, which always made his father smile. But every autumn a peculiar restlessness came over him, and he never felt warmth in his feet again. When he slept by the fire at night his eyes were always staring wide open.

After his father passed away Bradán became the sole guardian of the river and the people called him the Salmon Man. And I don't know what all Bradán did with the rest of his life, but I can tell you he married a local woman, and they had a family. They say his human descendants farmed in Glendun for a long time. But his salmon line still live, at least part of their lives, in the Brown River to this very day.

The Coaleyman and the Tinker's Daughter

For years untold fishermen from Islay in the Hebrides have sailed over the Sea of Moyle to Ireland with boat loads of salted coalfish or 'coaley', as it was called. These travelling fishermen were known as coaleymen.

They sold their goods as far south as Carrickfergus and Larne and all up through the Glens of Antrim. And at the end of the season, they pitched into Ballycastle for the Lammas Fair. They traded with travelling tinkers, and as their boats emptied of fish, they filled them up with tin pots and pans to take back to Islay and neighbouring Jura.

One year, young Stephen Cameron, just sixteen years old, set out from Port Ellen in his father's boat heading for Carrickfergus. With a favourable wind and the Paps of Jura falling away behind them, they made the crossing in a little under a dozen hours. Young Stephen was wide-eyed as they sailed into port. It was the first time he had ever left his home village of Ballygrant. He had never seen anything so wondrous as the great stone walls of the Norman Castle at Carrickfergus.

They tied up at the quay and unloaded their barrels of fish. His father renewed old acquaintances and introduced his son to many of them. Stephen never shook hands with so many strangers or heard so many strange tongues. Later in the day his father met with a tinker and greeted him warmly.

"This is my youngest laddie," he said.

"He must have the look of his mother," said the tinker. "He's far too handsome a lad to be a Cameron."

Young Stephen blushed, but mercifully the two men soon fell to reminiscing.

"You'll join us later," said the tinker, "for a bite of meat?"

"Aye, and I'll bring the whiskey," said Stephen's father.

That evening, Stephen and his father and his three older brothers walked out to where the tinkers were camped beyond the town. They met the tinker's wife and his three lovely daughters. The youngest was called Aoife. She was the same age as Stephen. Well, people talk about love at first sight, but when that young coaleyman laid eyes on the tinker's daughter his heart nearly went sideways in him.

Aoife's mother noticed that Stephen had an eye for her daughter. She was so taken by the handsome young fellow that she contrived to let the youngsters spent a little time together. Over the next day or two they held hands, and more than once they kissed each other on the lips.

We all know that feeling of first love. There's nothing like it. Nothing so pleasing or so painful in this whole world. Imagine then a week later when they had to part company. Aoife wept, and Stephen had to bite his lip so he wouldn't make a fool of himself. They held each other and vowed always to be true. They promised each other faithfully they would meet up at the Lammas Fair in Ballycastle at the end of summer.

All the way home young Stephen sat up near the bow and let the sea spray hide the tears that streamed down his young beardless face. His brothers tried to cheer him up with a bit of banter, but he was heartbroken, and their father bid them to lay off with their teasing.

"You'll see your wee tinker lass soon enough, laddie," his father said, but the young lad's spirits could not be raised.

Stephen counted the long slow days, but eventually the Lammas Fair came around once more. The coaleymen loaded up their boats to the gunwales and set sail for Ballycastle. Young Stephen was fit to burst. As soon as they had tied up and all the barrels were on the quay, his father let him run on. Stephen searched every place. He asked every tinker he met, but no one had seen or heard tell of Aoife or her family. By evening time he was so down in the doldrums that he just wanted to cry. Aoife had broken her promise.

"Agh, there could be a hundred reasons why they haven't come this year," his father scolded. "The world doesn't turn around Stephen Cameron you know."

But the young coleyman was too young and too lovesick to hear a word of sense.

By the end of the week the coaleymen had sold their fish and once again were loaded up with tinware. The time had come to say their farewells and return to Islay. It was only forty miles or so across the Sea of Moyle, but it might as well have been the far side of the world. Stephen's father saw the change in him.

"Are you coming hame, son?" he asked.

Stephen just shook his head. There was no point in trying to talk him out of staying, and neither did his father want them to part on bad terms.

"Then take this, laddie," and he gave Stephen a few shillings. "God knows what I'll have to listen to from your mother."

They passed Stephen's gear ashore with as much bread and cheese as he could carry. Stephen waved them off at the quay and as they sailed out of Ballycastle harbour his father said to his brothers, "He'll either sink or he'll swim now."

Overnight young Stephen became a man of the roads – an itinerant worker. His bread and cheese lasted a week and his silver a few months. He travelled from town to town in search of Aoife, but never found hilt nor hair of her. He got work from local farmers. He slept in their barns and byres and became well known and well liked throughout the countryside. Every August he would wend his way back to Ballycastle for the

Lammas Fair in the hope of finding Aoife, and to meet up with the coaleymen and hear news of Islay.

Time passed and Stephen's mother and father were buried in Kilmeny churchyard in their native parish. Stephen became an uncle many times over, and still he never went home. One wild winter's night he was traipsing along a coastal path towards Ballycastle town when he saw a light in the pitch blackness. He wondered at it, for he had been that way many times before and didn't remember there being a dwelling at this place. As he got closer, he could just see the outline of a big house.

He reached the front door and lifted the knocker. When a finely dressed gentleman answered, Stephen asked for some food and shelter. The gentleman bid him to enter, and Stephen found himself in a magnificent hall lit by flaming torches. There were logs blazing in a big open grate and a wolfhound slept by the hearth. A banqueting table was laid with the finest foods and wine, and only two chairs set.

"Eat and drink your fill, Stephen," said the gentleman.

Stephen wondered how the gentleman knew his name, but his curiosity never got the better of his hunger.

"Tell me your story," said the gentleman, and as Stephen ate and drank, he recounted the tale you have just read.

When he had finished, the gentleman lifted a candelabra and led Stephen up a grand staircase. He showed him into a chamber where stood a four-poster bed draped with heavy cloth and spread with the softest eider down. It was the most comfortable night's sleep Stephen ever had.

When he awoke the next morning, he was curled up under his tattered overcoat on the grass in among the ruins of an old castle, a few miles outside the town. The sea breeze was gently tugging at his hair. There was no magnificent hall, no fire, no wolfhound, no banquet and no finely dressed gentleman. It had all seemed so real, and yet it must have been a dream. Still and all, he was well-slept and his belly was full. Then he felt in his waistcoat pocket and found a little bag of gold sovereigns. He remembered what the gentleman had said.

"Tell no man how you came by this, and forget you ever saw me."

Well, Stephen went into town. He bought himself a new pair of brogues and a new overcoat. He treated himself to a dram or two of whiskey, and he noticed that his purse never seemed to lighten. He gave to the poor and made merry wherever he went. Of course, the people always wanted him to stay with them, so generous was he with his money and so entertaining with his songs and stories. But he never stayed anywhere for more than one night, so intent was he in his quest to find Aoife.

The following year, as usual, Stephen pitched up to the Lammas Fair at Ballycastle. He fortified himself with a dram or two, and as he walked through the crowded streets, he caught a glimpse of the finely dressed gentleman. In his excitement he hailed his old benefactor.

"Sir, sir. Do you remember me? It's Stephen Cameron. From Islay."

The gentleman turned around with a face like thunder.

"I warned you to forget you ever saw me. Where is the bag of gold sovereigns I gave you?"

Stephen pulled it from his pocket and held it out.

"Look inside."

As Stephen did so, the strange gentleman touched the bottom of the bag with his cane. The coins turned to autumn leaves and a cloud of dust came up into Stephen's eyes and blinded him.

The people said they had heard him talking to himself just before he fell to the ground. For years after that he was always known as the blind beggar. But the people whose lives he had touched never forgot his kindness. They would keep him for a night and then guide him along the road to the next farmhouse. By such goodwill he continued to travel around the countryside, always in the hope of finding Aoife.

And that's the story of the young Stephen Cameron, the coaleyman who fell in love with a tinker's daughter. As far as I know he never found Aoife. When he died years later, some of his young relatives from Islay ferried him back home. He was buried with his people in Kilmeny churchyard, where a stone of the local black marble was erected to mark his grave.

It's a sad story I suppose, but then again not too many people have known such a lifetime of devotion, for his was a true and faithful love. Far fewer folk have had a song written about them. You know the one …

I wish I was in Carrickfergus
Only for the nights in Ballygrant
I would swim over the deepest ocean
Just to see my love before I die
But the sea is wide and I cannot swim over
Nor have I wings that I might fly
I wish I could be once more a boatman
To ferry me over with my love to lie

Now in Kilmeny it is reported
On marble stones there as black as ink
With gold and silver I would support her
But I'll sing no more now till I've had a drink
Well I'm drunk today and I'm seldom sober
A handsome rover from town to town
Ah but I'm sick now my days are numbered
Come all ye young men and lay me down

The Golden Hare

Hugh Pat Molloy lived at the foot of Knocklayde Mountain in Glenstaise, which is near the town of Ballycastle. He was a deadly shot with a double-barrelled shotgun. Every Saturday in life he went over hill and dale with his wee spaniel dog and shot whatever flew up or ran out in front of him. His family never wanted for meat. They fed on all the wild game Hugh Pat brought home for the table.

Then, during one of England's wars, when the value of life was low and the price of food was high, Hugh Pat found he could make a few extra shillings with his gun. A game dealer came round once a week on a horse and cart and bought all the fur and feather Hugh Pat could shoot. He paid thruppence for a rook, sixpence for a pigeon, ninepence for a rabbit and a shilling for a big Irish hare. Everything was shipped to England to feed the folk over there.

Hugh Pat made more money for three or four hours on a Saturday than he made for a whole week's labour on the farm. But as he shot out one place after another, he had to go further and further. He took to shooting every wee bird he came across. Tasty and all as they were for making a pot of broth, there wasn't much meat on a snipe or a woodcock, and the game dealer didn't pay much for the likes of them.

It got to be the wee larks and thrushes weren't even safe. Hugh Pat shot everything that moved and a few things that didn't! His neighbours began to complain that he was destroying the whole countryside for miles around. They liked to hear the corncrake and the cuckoo and the curlew calling out their own names. They enjoyed the lapwing's mad sky dance and listening to the skylark chirruping all day long and the eerie bleating of the snipe at dusk. And they began to curse Hugh Pat Molloy for his foolishness and greed.

One evening, just as darkness was falling, Hugh Pat was standing by the side of a wood. Just then an owl flew out of the trees on long slow-flapping wings. He knew fine well it was no use for the pot and no value to the game dealer, but he hadn't raised a thing all day. The urge to shoot that owl was irresistible. He glanced over his shoulders this way and that, for his mother had always told him, 'No matter what you do son, if it's a sin, somebody will be watching you.' But sure, he was in the middle of nowhere – not a person would see him. He raised his shotgun and squeezed the trigger. The owl folded its wings and dropped like a stone.

Hugh Pat bid his spaniel to retrieve it. "Fetch it up boy."

But the dog put its tail between its legs and whined and cowed at his feet.

"What the devil's wrong with you, boy?" Hugh Pat said, but of course the wee dog never answered (it would have been an odd thing if it had). Well, Hugh Pat roared and shouted, but the more he did the more the dog shied away. He threatened to shoot the poor thing, but no matter what he said or did, the dog refused to retrieve the owl.

"What's the point of having a dog and barking yourself?" Hugh Pat muttered, and he stamped off to retrieve the owl himself.

As he was looking about where it fell, he nearly stood on a hare hiding down in among the rushes, with its ears lying flat along its back. Its coat was the colour of the setting sun, and its eyes were the fierce blue of a summer sky. Hugh Pat had heard stories about golden hares, but he had never seen one.

Just then it started up and loped away. Hugh Pat put the gun to his shoulder. He took aim and, BANG! The shot echoed away. The hare's back legs skittered sideways. Hugh Pat smiled to himself, for it was a good shot. But the hare was only hit by two or three pickles. It regained its balance and with a mighty turn of speed, jinked this way and that through the rushes, leaving nothing but a spray of evening dew in its wake.

Well, Hugh Pat threw down his gun and kicked the ground. He was raging with himself. You see, a wounded animal would only end up food for the fox or the raven – what the hunter called a dead loss. Hugh Pat's poor wife would have some complaining to listen to that evening, but when he got back home, wasn't she was waiting for him at the door.

"Holy Mother of God, Hugh Pat, what kept you so long? I've been worried sick." And Hugh Pat soon discovered the cause of his wife's dismay. "It's The wean," she said. "One minute he was happy as Larry and the next thing he just started bawling and crying and he won't stop."

The wean was what they called their youngest child. He was only eighteen months old, and he never gave a bit of bother. Ate like a horse and slept the clock around. Well, Hugh Pat took one look at the child. His skin was red as a beetroot and his wee face was wrinkled up like a cabbage leaf. In those days there was no such thing as running for a doctor. The only thing they could do was take him to Meabh Rua – Red Maeve, the wise woman.

Meabh Rua was so called for the colour of her long, wild hair. She was well known throughout the country. Some people whispered she was in league with the Good Folk, but that's what they always said about the wisest of wise women. Still in all, they called on her in times of need. She had delivered the wean – turned him in his mother's womb and untangled the cord from round his wee neck to give him life. She had little time for any man, be they priest or landlord. And for the likes of Hugh Pat Molloy, she had no time at all.

"You'll have to take the wean to Meabh Rua," said Hugh Pat to his wife. "Me and her have never seen eye to eye."

"Oh yes, you will come along," his wife said in that way that Hugh Pat knew was the last word. "I might need you."

So they carried the wean over the hill to Meabh Rua's cabin. She bid Hugh Pat to wait by the door and waved his wife and the child in nearer to the fire. Without hardly looking at him she said, "It's no fever, Mrs Molloy. Your son has fallen under an enchantment. Ask your husband if he knows the meaning of it."

"My husband? What would he know about it?"

"Ask him. He's standing there."

"Ask me what?" said Hugh Pat. "How would I know what's wrong with him?"

"Have you offended the Good Folk in any way?" demanded Meabh Rua.

"I've offended nobody," said Hugh Pat unconvincingly, and his wife knew him better.

"Hugh Pat Molloy, if you have anything to confess speak it now," she said.

"I have nothing to confess. If I did it would be to the parish priest!"

"You'll confess it here and now or you'll have the death of your son on your conscience. Did you kill an owl?" Meabh Rua cried.

"I shot an owl by mistake. But sure, what about it?"

Meabh Rua turned to Hugh Pat's wife. "As sure as night follows day, if your man does not repent, your child will die."

Hugh Pat wanted to ask how the devil Meabh Rua knew about that owl, but the words withered in his throat as he remembered what his mother had always told him. "No matter what you do son, if it's a sin, somebody will be watching you."

"What must we do?" asked Mrs Malloy.

"Take his gun to the blacksmith in the village. The barrels must be heated in the forge until they're white hot. They must be beaten into the shape of a cross on the anvil. On this he must swear never to harm another living thing. When that's done, bring the cross to me."

Well, that's what happened. Hugh Pat was marched home and from there to the blacksmith, who carried out Meabh Rua's instructions to the letter. Hugh Pat's wife made him swear on the cross and, just to be sure, the Good Book as well, that he would never harm another living thing.

While she followed at a discreet distance to make sure he carried out her instructions, Mrs Malloy made her man deliver the metal cross to Meabh Rua. When Hugh Pat reached her cabin he was about to knock on her door, but he stopped short, for he could hear her singing. He peeped through a crack in the timbers. Meabh Rua was sitting on a stool by the fire with her skirts pulled up. In a basin of water she was bathing wounds on the back of her leg – three or four wee holes from which a little blood seeped. And all the while she sang a little song.

Hugh Pat Molloy that fool
of a man

Would kill all the Good
Folk in Erin's green land

Would it not be far better
if he drowned in the sea

And spared his poor wife
and his young family.

And then suddenly she spun round on the stool. In the fire light her hair seemed to blaze like the setting sun. Her eyes, the fierce blue of a summer sky, burned right through that door into Hugh Pat's thumping heart. In that moment he realised that Meabh Rua and the golden hare were one and the same. It was true, after all – she was in league with the Good Folk. Hugh Pat dropped the cross with a clatter and a clang and he ran back home for his dear life.

Well, the wean mended up and grew into a fine young man. As far as I know, Hugh Pat Molloy was true to his oath. He never harmed another living thing for the rest his life. They say from that to his dying day the only thing he would ever let over his lips was spuds and buttermilk.

The Rathlin Farmer

On his twenty-first birthday John McIntyre inherited the small family farm on Rathlin Island. His father always used to say, "One cow would thrive on it, two would survive but three would starve."

His birthday coincided with the Lammas Fair in Ballycastle, and now that he had come of age, he thought he would take himself across to the mainland for a bit of craic. So the following day he spruced himself up and sailed over on the morning tide.

When he got up into the town there were card trick men, fortune tellers, tinkers, hawkers, and fiddlers and pipers at every pub door. There were boys running horses up and down the main street and crowds of folk everywhere, dealing and drinking and dancing.

John wasn't there two minutes when he spied the most beautiful young girl he had ever seen. Her skin was sun-burnished, and she had the daintiest wee waist. Her long black hair was tied back in a ponytail, and whatever way the August sun caught it now and then it shimmered like a rook's wing. John fell into a kind of a trance.

Just by that he heard someone call, "Nancy, Nancy." And the next thing, she skipped across the street in her bare feet to an older man John took to be her father. All day John followed them. When they stopped, he stopped, when they moved on, he moved on. But how and ever, eventually John got close enough and brave enough to speak to her.

"Are you sellin' horses, miss?" he asked.

"My grandfather is," she answered. "If he gets a good price the morrow we might stay for another day or two."

When Nancy's grandfather turned around John took off his cap and said, "Hello, sir. Would you be wantin' any help to lead your horses up and down the street?"

The old man looked John up and down. "We're camped out along the commons. Sure, come with us for a bite of supper?"

Nancy and her grandfather were travelling people, John knew that straight off. And like all the old travelling people, if you were a guest of theirs you were treated like a king. That night they dined on the best of rabbit stew. The meat just melted in John's mouth, and he thought he'd never tasted anything like it in his life.

"It's the open air," the old man said. "Everything tastes better – food, water, whiskey, even the air itself." By that he took out a bottle of crystal clear poitín. "Do you know what this is?" he said to John.

"I do, sir," John replied.

"Well," says he, "let's drink to the open air and the open road."

And him and John fell to drinking the bottle of poitín. Then the old traveller took out a fiddle and began to play. John listened, his eyes dancing in his head and his feet tapping in time to the jig.

When the tune was over the old man said, "Give us a song or a story, young fella."

And John began to sing.

The people were saying, that no two e'er were wed
But one had a sorrow that never was said
And she smiled as she passed by with her goods and her gear,
And that was the last that I saw of my dear.

John could sing alright, but when Nancy joined in they made the most beautiful music together. She could sing like a blackbird, and whether it was the poitín or the exquisite natural harmonies or what, big silent tears rolled down the old man's ruddy cheeks.

Well, they were up at the crack of dawn the next morning and Nancy fried them all herrings in oatmeal. They brushed the animals down and combed out their manes and their tails. They mixed grease from the skillet with soot from the pots and blackened their hooves. The camp was tidied, their faces were given a lick, and they led the horses back into the town. John ran them up and down the street two or three times each in front of the seemingly disinterested dealers. There was a lot bantering back and forward, hand slapping and spitting, but eventually all the dealing was done and the horses were led away by their new owners.

When they had their fill of the fair, they went back to their campsite for a bite of supper. When they had eaten there was a song or two, but Nancy's grandfather was tired.

"I'm for bed," he said. "Morning comes quickly. Don't be sitting too late now, Nancy. We'll have to make an early start."

John felt a wave of desperation break over him. Even before he could get to know Nancy properly, she was going to be leaving him. But somehow a wee spark must have jumped out of that fire and into their young hearts. Nancy's grandfather couldn't have turned in his bed before the two young lovers fell into each other's arms. And all night they lay together under that beautiful clear Lammas sky.

They awoke the next morning as naked as the day they were born, with only an old horse blanket to save their modesty. The fire was out, the pots and pans were gone, the caravan was gone, and Nancy's grandfather was gone. They pulled on their clothes in a hurry. When John felt a weight in his waistcoat pocket, he put his fingers in and pulled out a wee leather purse. Inside there were about two dozen gold sovereign coins.

"What's this?" he said to Nancy, but she was past herself with guilt and shame and annoyance.

Eventually she said, "It's my dowry. My grandfather has left it for you."

John didn't know where he was or what to say. He had never seen so much money in his life. He tried to give it over to Nancy, but she wouldn't take it. All day they searched the town but found no trace of the old traveller. By evening time, John realised there was nothing for it, but that Nancy would have to sail over the sound and back home to Rathlin with him.

He knew the folk would be talking, but he didn't care. He knew his mother would be pulling her hair out, but a team of horses wouldn't have dragged him away from Nancy now. Call it love or lust or whatever you like, but John was head over heels. And Nancy, well, it was obvious the way she looked at him that she was just as struck by love.

Time passed, and John doubted it was possible to be happier – until, that was, May Eve the following year, when Nancy gave birth to a lovely wee six pound baby girl. She was the image of her mother, so there was nothing else to do but call her Nancy too. Great precautions were taken with the infant. Fire tongs were placed over her cradle, and twisted wreaths of rowan were hung over the threshold to ward off the faerie folk, for it was that time of the year when they caused most mischief.

No harm came to the child, and the little family might have lived happily ever after, but there was one small fly in the ointment. John had noticed that as Nancy came nearer her time, she became very distant and weepy. "Agh, it's only natural," the older men told John as they worked the in the fields. "Women always turn a wee bit thrawn around the birth time. Sure it's just the same wie' a cow in calf."

For a while that contented John, but as time went on Nancy got more and more distant. And then John started waking up at night, and the bed clothes would be pulled back and Nancy would be gone. When he went to look for her, she would be out across the beach looking over to Ballycastle. John never disturbed her for he feared she might be walking in her sleep, and he had heard it was dangerous to wake someone like that. Eventually he spoke to his mother about it.

"Agh, John son, can you no' see what's happenin'?"

John shook his head.

"Nancy's fretting away like a bird in a cage. She's a traveller. She's never stayed in the same place more than a week or two, until now. Island life is no life for someone like Nancy, son."

John had always looked to his mother for the answers to all life's difficult questions. "What can I do, Ma?"

With a long sigh his mother said, "When your father was alive he used to trap the wee linnets and keep them in a cage in the scullery, and they would sing all summer long. But after a while they stopped singing and eating, and their feathers drooped, and he knew if he didn't let them go they would die."

And that was all she said.

When August came and the hay was in, John said to Nancy, "The Lammas Fair's on next week in Ballycastle. Maybe your grandfather will be up again. We could take wee Nancy over to meet him, eh?"

Well, Nancy bounced out of the chair. She threw her arms around John and the life seemed to come back into her. And so when the time came, John got them all into the boat and sailed over to Ballycastle. When he tied up on the quay, he told Nancy he had forgot to do some chore or other and that he would have to return to the island. He kissed his baby daughter, and to Nancy he gave the purse of gold sovereigns.

"If you see anything at all for you or the wean, treat yourselves," he said. "I'll come back over this evening and sure maybe we'll stay a day or two if ye like."

And that was the last time they ever laid eyes on one another. John moped about the island for two or three years, but when his mother passed away, he could stick it no longer. He sold up to a neighbour for a pittance and headed over to the mainland. He took a wee cottage at Murlough Bay and lived like a hermit, rarely speaking to another living soul. But every Lammas tide he would make the long walk across the boulder field at the foot of the cliffs and up the Grey Man's Path, along Fair Head and down into the town.

Seventeen years passed, and the Lammas Fair came round again. When John looked out the door of his cottage there was big sea mist rolling in and the rain was starting to fall. "Maybe it'll have fared by the morning," he thought to himself.

Next day the weather had cleared enough, and John made the trek up over Fair Head. When he got to the top, breathing hard from the near-vertical climb, he took a minute to catch his second wind. He glanced over and saw a single white swan gliding across the glassy waters of Lough-na-Cranagh. Then, out the side of his eye, he noticed something over at the edge of the cliff. It was a shawl. John crept over to the edge on all fours and peered down the sheer wall of basalt. Four hundred feet below at the base of the cliff was a sprawling figure.

It took a while to pick his way back down. When he got there, he turned the broken body over. Battered and bruised as it was, he recognised his beautiful teenage daughter instantly, for she was the image of her mother when she was that age.

It transpired she'd arrived in the town the day before and enquired everywhere for John McIntyre. Eventually a publican told her where she might find her father but warned her not to go up over Fair Head in the dark and the mist. In her desire to find her father, young Nancy had ignored the advice and paid for her impetuousness with her young life.

John McIntyre took his daughter over to his native island and buried her in along with his mother. Not very long after he followed her into that same grave – died of a broken heart, they said.

Years later an Englishman on a walking tour of the Glens got benighted on Fair Head and very wisely chose to camp beside Lough-na-Cranagh. When he came down into Ballycastle the next day, he said that the whole night long he could hear a young girl singing the most beautiful song he'd ever heard. Of course, the locals knew all about the wee girl that sings up on Fair Head at night when the sea mist is in. So if ever you should find yourself up there at night and you hear her, don't be afraid. It's only young Nancy McIntyre singing for her father.

She stepped away from me as she moved through the fair
And fondly I watched her move here and move there
Then she went her way homeward with one star awake
As the swan in the evening moves over the lake

The Rathlin Mermaid

A good many years ago a couple lived in the Glens of Antrim. He was born and bred, a Cushendall man, but she was a runner-in from Rathlin Island. Their children were all up and away long ago, and to help keep hearth and home together the woman let a spare room to the occasional lodger.

One day a young woman came to their door. "I hear you take in lodgers," she said. "Have you a spare room just now?"

She had long hair the colour of fresh straw and pale, turquoise-blue eyes. Her lips were thin and shapeless, and another odd thing the landlady noticed about her was that she seemed to have no fingernails. Well, the landlady thought she was a timid little thing but harmless for all that, and so she showed her the room.

"Three shillings a week, board and keep, and that's cheap. You'll not get better around here for love nor money," said the landlady.

The young woman accepted and moved in right away.

She was easy enough to look after. Every morning she went out and never came back till evening. The landlady offered her spuds and cabbage and bacon and tea and goats milk, but all she would eat was a small piece of the salt fish that hung on a nail at the back of the door, and to wash it down a glass of spring water in which she always put a pinch of salt. After her meal she would go into her room, and they wouldn't see hide nor hair of her till next morning. She gave no bother except that where she left her button boots by the door there was always a dusting of fine sand, which the landlady brushed up every night before bedtime.

Every Friday evening the landlady's husband lifted his fiddle and went away to the local public house to ceilidh with his friends or, under the light of a full moon, to play for the dancers at the crossroads away out of the village and far from the prying eyes of the local priest. Then the landlady would bring in a big tin bath to the fire and fill it for her guest.

But when she went to boil a pan of water over the fire for the bath, the young woman said, "Don't go to any bother for me, missus, cold water will do fine."

"It's no bother, dear," said the landlady. "You can't be bathing in cold water. You'll get your death."

But the young woman insisted, and so the bath was filled with icy water straight from the pump.

"Could you spare a wee pinch or two of salt, missus?"

"Certainly," said the landlady.

When the salt was dusted into the bath she turned, and there was the young woman standing stark naked and not the slightest bit concerned. The landlady averted her eyes and busied herself at the other end of the kitchen. But every now and again she glanced over her shoulder to watch the antics of her guest. The young woman splashed and scooped the water up and threw it over herself and all about the place. She laughed and played in the bath with all the abandon of a small child.

The landlady had never seen anything like it. To her great surprise, she also noticed that although the young woman was full-breasted, she seemed to have no nipples, and neither had she a belly button! Of course, the landlady made no comment, but after an hour or so she called, "You'll be catching your death in that cold water, dear."

When the maiden stepped from the bath she never shivered. Nor did she even attempt to dry herself. She just pulled on her clothes and away she went straight into her room and closed the door.

Late that night the landlady's husband came home and found his wife wide awake. "What in under God has you up at this hour?"

"Wait till you hear what I witnessed this night," said the landlady, and she told him all about the strange goings-on in every tiny detail. By the time she had finished, her husband was fast asleep and not a word of sense could she get out of him.

Next morning nothing was mentioned until the young woman went out as usual. No sooner had the latch clicked on the door than the landlady said to her husband, "Do you mind a word of what I told you last night?"

"I do, of course," said he.

"Well, what do you think?"

"About what?"

"About her antics, bathing in the cold water and such."

"Agh, I think what odds if she wants to bath in cold water. If she wants to bath in cow's milk let her, as long as she pays for it, mind."

"Aye, but what about her breasts and all that?"

The landlady's husband sighed, for his head was sore and he had no interest in his wife's blethering.

"D'ye want to know what I think?" said the woman, her eyes darting round the room. "I think … I think she's a mermaid?"

"A what? Have you lost your mind altogether, woman? Would ye give me peace." The landlady's husband had heard enough. He rose from the table and went out for a walk to clear his head.

Well, the weeks went past and nothing much more was mentioned. But being a Rathlin Islander, the landlady knew all about mermaids, for there are more mermaids – or sea maidens, call them what you will – around the shores of Rathlin than anywhere else in Ireland. She was sure she was right, and to convince her husband she took an idea in her head.

The following Friday she said to him, "Go you out as usual tonight but come back in half an hour. I'll turn up the lamp in the kitchen and leave the curtain back in the window, and you'll see for self what I'm talking about."

While the bath was being prepared the maiden began to undress. When she stood there stark naked, the landlady could hold her tongue no longer.

"Miss," she said, "please don't be offended, but I cannae help notice that you have no nipples."

"Nipples? What are they?" said the wee maiden.

"You know, for feeding a wean."

But the young woman looked bewildered.

"Nipples is where the milk comes from …"

Still there was not the slightest flicker of understanding. So the landlady unbuttoned her gansy and bared up her own large bosom.

"Your breasts should be like this, dear," she said. "These are called nipples – you know – for nursing a baby."

But it was obvious the young woman hadn't the slightest notion what the woman was talking about.

Then the landlady said, "And you've no belly button either."

"Belly button – what's that?"

The landlady pointed to her midriff, "You know, your navel."

In complete exasperation the woman rolled her skirts up and tucked them under her chin. She reached in under the folds and pulled down her big kidney warmers. "That's your belly button," she said pointing at her navel, but the young woman looked even more bewildered and none the wiser.

The landlady pulled her undergarments down further still and pointed to her own nether regions. "The baby comes out here – and don't even start me about it how gets in there in the first place – but when it's born, the mother is still attached by a sort of a cord to the wean's belly. When it's cut it slowly dries up and falls off, and that leaves a wee scar. That's your belly button, but you don't have one!"

With that the maiden burst into tears. She ran in to the landlady's arms, who had no time to cover up her bare breasts and readjust her undergarments. It took a long time to pacify the young woman but eventually she confessed that she was indeed a mermaid.

"I was caught by an old fisherman near Rathlin," she said. "He was a cruel and ill-tempered master, but mercifully he soon died. He left me all the wealth he had gathered up throughout his long, miserable oul life. But all I want is my tail back. Without it I can never return to the sea."

The landlady wanted to shout out "I knew it!" but she let the young woman tell her story.

"The fisherman took my tail and hid it to make me live among humans. Every day I search far and wide for it. It must exist somewhere, for if it had been destroyed I would already be dead."

Later that night the landlady's husband came home. He'd taken a wee bit more drink than usual, but when he got into bed beside his wife she said excitedly, "Well did you see?"

"Aye, I seen," he said irritably.

"Well, now do you see what I mean about her?"

"Aye, I seen her."

"But did you see everything?"

"I did, and I saw the bloody exhibition you made of yourself."

"What do you mean?" said she.

"I mean what I say. I was never so ashamed in my life – you, showing your breasts and all for the whole bloody world to see."

"It's nothing you haven't seen before," she said, "but if you want to be like that it'll be a long time before you see it again." The landlady turned in the bed and bid her husband a frosty goodnight.

The next day she went to Rathlin to consult the wisest old woman on the island, for she suspected that the fisherman would have sought her counsel before attempting to catch a mermaid. Sure enough, she was right. The wise woman knew the whole story, and happily she agreed to help the young woman.

To cut a long story short, the mermaid was reunited with her tail. She went straight back into the sea and was ever more cautious of boats and humans. She left the landlady all the money bequeathed her by the fisherman for, as she said herself, she would have no need of it in the ocean.

The landlady and her husband lived quite comfortably from that day on, and they never again had to take in a lodger. The husband quit his Friday night ceilidh sessions and hung his fiddle on the wall. Anytime mention was made of the strange young woman he fell into an old bad humour and stamped out of the house.

As far as I know, the landlady went to her grave not knowing why her man was always so vexed at the mere mention of the mermaid. You see, I don't think he ever told her that the night she turned the lamp up in the kitchen and left the curtain back for her husband to see, the whole bloody ceilidh band was there too.

Cloch Mhór Fhearghusa

In ancient times there was a young man called Fergus Mhór. He was the son of a humble clansman, and as his name suggested he was large of stature and strong of limb.

Even in the days before bronze and iron blades were brought to Ireland, conflict swept back and forth over the land like the ebb and flow of the tide. Clansmen clashed with their neighbours over things now long forgotten. Settlements and alliances were brokered. Marriages were arranged. Women lived short and often brutal lives. Men died in bloody battle fighting for their chieftain's gain and their clan's honour. And so, when Fergus Mhór came of age, like all the other young men of his clan, he was destined to become a warrior.

Some men dreaded to leave their home place where they had gathered hazel nuts in the woods or speared salmon in the river. The fear of never more returning to a loved one haunted their every dream. But others relished the prospect of glory; of becoming heroes whose great deeds would be told and retold around flickering cooking-fires to ardent fish-eyed listeners for generations to come.

As for Fergus Mhór he neither shrunk from nor took delight in the thought of becoming a warrior. It was just something that had to be braved. He had been blessed with a fine physique and striking features but more important was his composure and clearness of mind. Given the choice, he would have preferred to stay at home and marry the young woman to whom he had been betrothed. He had great hopes of becoming a faithful husband and fathering many sons and daughters. But so had countless other young warriors before him.

In his growing up Fergus Mhór had seen enough of life and death to not be fooled into thinking he was invincible. His father had often told him about the horrors of war. Many of his kith and kin had not returned from battle or had come back broken and disturbed men.

In those days of long ago it was customary for warriors entering the field of battle to cast a stone upon a heap and, if they survived, to retrieve it afterwards. By such means a tally was kept of those warriors lost. Over time these stones became a mark of endurance. For a warrior to be eventually buried with his tally stone grasped in his hand, was to prove to the guardians of the otherworld that he had fought in many battles and deserved his place among the ancestors.

Well, Fergus Mhór was by nature a hopeful young man and far-sighted beyond his years. Every undertaking was entered into wholeheartedly, every question considered deeply. And so, as he prepared for his first foray onto the battlefield and was told to find himself a tally stone, he did not just lift the first white pebble that came to his hand. He struck out along the beach where his clansmen were encamped looking for the perfect stone.

He weighed and pored over lumps of quartz and flint rounded by countless tides. He judged their fit in his hand and held the cold, sea-smoothed surfaces to his lips. But none seemed to please him – at least not entirely. The older warriors began to nudge each other as they watched his antics. Fergus Mhór was oblivious for he was too busy with the task in hand. Eventually he found a stone that seized his attention. It was much bigger than the egg-sized pebbles the other men seemed to favour. It was a cobblestone the size of his own clenched fist.

As he returned to where the men were taking their ease feasting on shellfish and mead before the battle, they baited him. "Are you sure that stone's big enough there, Fergus? Maybe we could lend you a hand or yoke up an ox to the cart to get a bigger one." There were bawls of laughter, but Fergus Mhór took their harmless mockery with his usual good grace.

And then he raised the stone to reveal a hole the size of a man's finger that ran straight through its core. He held the stone up to his eye and peered through the opening. Everyone fell silent for they knew Fergus Mhór had found a rare and much sought-after hag stone. These special stones were long known to be possessed of great power. Through one, a man of knowledge or a spae wife might catch a glimpse of a place and a time beyond the here and now. As he stood there looking through the hole, Fergus Mhór was suddenly awake to the great suffering and violence that was to follow, but he was also gripped with the powerful sense that he would not be slain in battle.

In a world long out of mind where druids and strange gods held sway, the emblem of a favourite deity held power enough to dispel misfortune. The tusk of a boar or the canine of a wolf could imbue the wearer with the animal's strength and courage. It was a cherished talisman that could fortify a warrior's resolve on the battlefield and perhaps afford some otherworldly protection. Such a possession was more dearly held than any be-jewelled trinket. Fergus Mhór found his good luck charm that day on the beach. Heavy as it was, he carried his stone with him everywhere and when he placed it on the tally heap before battle everyone knew to whom it belonged. They called it Cloch Mhór Fhearghusa – Big Fergus' Stone.

Fergus Mhór survived that first battle when a dozen of his clansmen did not. He came home to wed the young woman to whom he had been betrothed and they started their family. He endured many more battles and skirmishes in the years that followed. The vile taste of bloodshed never left his mouth easily, but when he held the hag stone in his hand and looked through the hole, as he did often, some voice deep within him always spoke of old age. And though he was never careless on the field of battle, neither did he fret for his own mortality.

Comrades sensed his strength and rallied about him. They were moved to shield him, and some even gave their lives that he might carry on the fight. Fergus Mhór became his clan's living talisman – their emblem of endurance and hope. Sitting around the cooking-fires at night they begged him to peer through his hag stone their fortunes to foretell. He always found some gentle way of lifting their spirits and dulling their fears.

Time passed and Fergus Mhór became their clan chief. He lived to be a very old and wise leader. When he eventually died, he was buried amid great sorrow and ritual. They fetched up a heavy flat stone and laid it over four or five uprights that had been heaved into place. In this simple, hard-wrought chamber they placed his body. Around him they arranged a few things that had defined him in life. Then the tomb was heaped over with a great cairn of white tally stones, so that the guardians of the otherworld might know that the warrior whose spirit came to them was their much-loved and lamented chieftain, Fergus Mhór.

In the many centuries since then the cairn has been picked clean. All that now remains of Fergus Mhór's tomb is a few weather-beaten standing stones aslant on a lonely, windswept hillside overlooking the Sea of Moyle. The dust of his bones has long since blown away on the breeze. No written word chronicles his life and times, but the people told his story – father to son – for generations until only a few echoes and whispers of it could be heard.

But in the shallow earth, together with a few ancient shards of pottery and beads, his most cherished possession endured … Cloch Mhór Fhearghusa – Big Fergus' Stone.

Cuilén Bán

A runner-in to our townland the neighbours said was daft,
Some of them even whispered he dabbled at witchcraft.
They scared themselves with stories about the bogeyman
Who lived in the house beside the moss where a brown burn
    ran.

Now Cuilén Bán was a rare boy it's only fair to say
But in the most delightful and soul-enriching way.
A man of many insights, as far as a mind could see,
He knew the song of every bird, the leaf of every tree.

He knew each and every star and he watched them through a
    glass
He didn't care if people thought there was wiser eating grass.
He talked about Cassiopeia, The Pleiades and Gemini
He said the greatest show on earth was a clear night sky.

He was a child of the universe, devoted from the first,
A son of mother nature, for knowledge an unquenchable thirst.
The dawn chorus was music to his ears, he found drama
    everywhere
When he watched a falcon stooping or a plover clap the air.

He took delight in the fox cubs rolling around their den
A tragedy in his book was a pack of hunting men.

He used to take in orphans and strays and waifs of every kind
There were badgers, hares and jackdaws, and once an owl that
    was blind.

Caterpillars and tadpoles, the miracle to observe,
Stood on a shelf by the window, his curiosity to serve.
He thought spiders and beetles the most mesmerizing of all
The way he let them run up his arm made my skin crawl.

He could lift a trout from the river with nothing more than his
    hand,
But said he couldn't bring himself to fry wee the thing in the
    pan.
He lived on soda bread and eggs and the hens he kept them for
Were better fed nor he was and they laid in a kitchen drawer.

He collected things like a magpie, everything caught his eye.
He had fossils and rocks that sparkled, treasures no money could
    buy.
He had stones the shape of an arrow some boy had made from
    a flint.
I forget how many thousands of years he said since they were
    spent.

He had wee bird's nests and seashells, even the skull of a crow
And a thing he called a meteorite he said he found in the snow.
The stuff that man had, he could have opened a county museum
But I was one of the very few that ever came to see him.

Oh he was a real eccentric in every sense of the word,
In all my life, before or since, the likes I never heard.
He came off with wonderful stories, written by old dead
    Greeks,
He never told the same one twice and I called every week.

I heard about Finn McCool and his deer hounds Bran and
    Sceolang,
And yarns about banshees and faeries left me feared to walk
    home.
Yes, Cuilén Bán was a rare one, of that there can be no doubt
But every man has a shadow, in that he can't be left out.

Once a year in May he fell into an old dark humour.
They said he mourned a loved one, let it be truth or rumour.
For a week he never ate nor drunk, except for his homemade
    wine,
And dreary it was to see him not sitting up on cloud nine.

He lost his sense of wonder, he became a different man,
Just sat there day after day with a sore head in his hands.
But sooner or later the weather always loses its grip,
Ask any old farming man or the captain of any ship.

Cuilén Bán would soon get up and tend his honey bee hives
And start to take an interest again in the wee creatures' lives.
And then you'd see him out walking, a switch of grass in his
    mouth,
His head up and his eyes closed and his face turned to the south.

Then one year he vanished – like the corncrake he never came
    back.
The neighbours whispered agreement, Cuilén Bán was bound
    to crack.
They searched for him high up and low, in every hole in the
    moss
And they quizzed me and everyone they happened to come
    across.

Of Cuilén Bán they found no trace and I never told on him.
They probably think he's lying somewhere the rig of a
    skeleton.
And God only knows but maybe by now that could be the case,
But when I hear the folk talking it's hard to keep a straight face.

When they say, "He was took by the faeries," I just have to
    laugh
For them very same folk had the cheek to say Cuilén Bán was
    daft.
I never bat an eyelid when they say, "He must have drowned
    at sea."
For I don't want to let slip the secret he trusted to me.

His house of curiosities is gathering dust where they sit,
In a letter left on the dresser he gifted me every bit.
I haven't the heart for changes, I watch for him on the lane.
I know I'm wasting my time, but I keep watch just the same.

Whiles I imagine him walking on a lonely western strand
And the whole bloody world to himself and miles and miles of
    sand.
But now I think I'll be quiet, lest I give Cuilén Bán away.
Maybe I will sometime, but forgive me, it won't be the day.

The Disbelieving Farmer

Not that long ago in Ireland it used to be the custom that the ploughing did not start until after the last potatoes had been gathered in. From November onwards the stubble was ploughed and harrowed, the wheat and the barley fields were ploughed and only then, as long tradition dictated, the first potatoes were sown on St. Patrick's Day – the 17th of March.

For the poor old working horses it was the hardest time of the year. But there was always a lull during those shortest days of winter when the farmers kept Christmas and marked the turning of another year. While the people feasted, the animals could rest for a few days and fatten up on sweet summer hay and oats before the new year started.

But there was once a miserable old farmer who never kept any high-days or holy-days. He didn't believe in all that old nonsense. For him time was money, and every penny was a prisoner. He worked every hour that God sent and even refused to rest on the Sabbath. Christmas time was no different. He toiled away all through the season, and so too did his poor old working horses. Their shoulders were all harness sores with the constant rubbing of the big leather collars, and their ribs were sticking out through their hides for want of a wee bit of rest and good feeding.

Now in those days everyone knew that at midnight on Christmas Eve a very strange thing happened. You see when Jesus was born on that first Christmas Eve in that wee stable in Bethlehem the animals bore witness to the miracle of his birth. On that night, farm animals the world over were granted the power of human speech for an hour, so that they might spread the news that Christ was born. Ever since, at midnight on Christmas Eve, dumb animals have been able to speak.

Now countryfolk in Ireland were always sorely tempted to eavesdrop on their animal's conversations, but they knew that terrible misfortune would befall anyone who did. For fear they might overhear the animals speaking by chance, men of the road and hired labourers would rather have slept out in the fields, no matter the weather. No one dared bed down in barn, byre or stable on Christmas Eve night!

The miserable old farmer paid no heed to all these foolish superstitions. He didn't believe in them. He worked away from early morning to late at night. Many a time he was still cleaning hen eggs or feeding pigs long after the neighbours had retired for the evening. The older he got the less sleep he seemed to need and the longer hours he worked.

His two big, fine, strapping sons, however, never lifted a finger. They never had to for their father thought no one could do any job as well as himself. And so, he done all the chores about the place. The neighbour folk used to say that by the time his sons got their hands on the farm they would be rich men – idle rich men.

Well, this particular Christmas Eve the farmer was working late and, as always, he had no idea of the time. Just after midnight he went forward to the barn door, but he stopped in his tracks for he heard strange voices. Thinking it was thieves or the like, he tiptoed forward by the light of a hurricane lamp, and what he saw and heard sent the shivers down his spine. His two big horses were talking away to one another.

"That oul blert will work himself to death," said the oldest one.

"Aye, and us with him," replied the other.

"Ah, don't you worry. He'll be dead and buried before the spring."

"D'ye think so?"

"I know so, and that's when the fun'll start."

"The fun?" asked the younger horse.

"Mark my words, a tight gathering makes a wide scattering. Them two good-for-nothin' sons of his will squander every penny their oul da has salted away."

Well, there was a lot more said, but to cut a long story short, that was the gist of it. The farmer went in home, his face was as white as a sheet.

"You're finished early the night," said his wife. "Are you sickening for something?"

But the farmer never answered her. He just went on into his bed. And there he lay for a few days, thinking he was about to drop dead at any minute.

Well, he never, and eventually he swung his legs out of bed. He could see a wee stretch in the mornings, the length of a cock's crow, with every day that passed. The mistle thrushes were starting to sing and that gave him a bit of heart. By the first week of January, he was up and at the ploughing again – working his poor horses to the bone. The more time passed the less he thought about the events of that Christmas Eve night. Soon they left his mind altogether.

By the second week of March the ploughing was near all done, and on St. Patrick's Day he sowed an acre of spuds. That evening while the farmer was wheeling a heavy barrow of dung to the midden, didn't he take a pain in his heart and collapse. The doctor was sent for and then his clergyman but by dawn the farmer lay dead.

Well, such a send-off his two sons gave him. The neighbours had never seen a wake like it. There were barrels of porter, whiskey, pipes and tobacco, hocks of ham and as much bread and cheese as would have fed an army. Three days and nights they drunk and ate and smoked and played games. And on the 20th of March they buried the miserable old farmer. According to Old Moore's Almanac for that year, the first day of spring was the 21st of March. Just as his old horse had predicted, his master was dead and buried before the spring.

Before a year went by, the two sons had drunk and gambled away every single penny of their inheritance. Bit by bit the wee farm, animals and all, had to be sold off to pay their debts. The two horses went to a kindly neighbour, and they spent the rest of their days chewing sweet grass and oats at their leisure.

And that's the story of the miserable old farmer who heard his animals speak one Christmas Eve. So, if you've any sense, you'll take my advice! On Christmas Eve stay well away from barns, byres and stables. Make sure you're tucked up safe and sound well before midnight. And don't forget to believe in the spirit of Christmas. Keep it well and be merry.

A Christmas Miracle

Many long years ago there was a blacksmith whose name was Tom. He lived in a place called Glenravel – the Tenth Glen, as it is sometimes known. One Christmas Eve morning he got up and saw that it had snowed during the night. And now it was freezing hard as iron. The last of the peat had burned down in the hearth and it was bitterly, bitterly cold.

Tom hadn't worked for months after a big heavy horse had broken his arm. Of course, in those days if you didn't work you didn't eat. Anyway, his poor wife was trying to scrape together what she could to feed their four children, but there was neither flour to bake bread nor peats to rekindle the fire. It looked as though they were going to have a hard Christmas.

Tom pulled on his old, tattered overcoat and with his wife and children watching him through hungry, desperate eyes, he set out to walk the few miles into Ballymena town. In truth he did not know what he was going to do when he got there, but he couldn't just sit and watch his children grow hungrier and hungrier.

When he got into the town the people were busy getting ready for their own Christmases. The bakers and the poulterers and the butchers were working from well before dawn to long after dusk. Errand boys were running about from pillar to post. The smells of baking bread and roasting meats made Tom's stomach groan and grumble for the want something to eat.

Well, he got himself positioned on the busiest street corner and he held out his hand to the mercy of the passers-by. "Please, sir. Please, Mrs. I have four weans at home and nothing for them to eat. Please, could you spare a ha'penny." But no one could. He barely got a kindly look. Tom stood there with his hand out from morning till night and not a single copper crossed his palm.

The hustle and the bustle began to die down as folk made their way home to their families and their fires. Tom the blacksmith had no option but to head for Glenravel. It hadn't thawed all day, but now that the stars were out it was so cold he could barely feel his hands or his feet. His teeth were chattering uncontrollably, and his breath hung on the dense air like clouds of thick smoke. Tom began the weary trudge in the direction of home. Every step of the way he dreaded seeing the pinched, anxious faces of his children and his poor, long-suffering wife. Truth be told, if he could have taken an easier way out, he would have.

After a few miles, a snow flurry came on. It wasn't heavy but Tom was so exhausted from the cold and hunger that he lay down at the back of a hedge-ditch to take shelter. As he lay there, his shivering stopped. A strange warmth began to spread throughout his body, and he loosened his coat from about his neck. A kind of euphoria came over Tom and all care and worry left him. He closed his eyes to sleep; a sleep from which he may never have awakened. God knows how long he lay there like that, but then suddenly he heard the sharp crying of a baby, and the sobs of a woman in distress and he was stirred from his reverie. Reluctantly he came to his senses and felt the cold once more.

Tom listened intently. There was no mistaking it. A woman was in some distress nearby. He followed the sounds as they carried through the still, cold air. A couple of field lengths away he came across her – a young woman, little more than a girl, in fact. She had just given birth to a little baby boy who was lying bloody and naked in the snow between her legs. In those days it wasn't rare for young women in trouble to have unwanted babies out in the fields away from the prying eyes of neighbours. God only knows how many babies were born and then buried by their mothers, desperate to hide their shame.

Well, Tom took off his old tattered overcoat and wrapped up the mother and child in it. He tried to comfort her as best he could, but there was so little he could do.

"I'll go and get help," he said. "You stay here."

The young woman didn't look like she was in any position to go anywhere, and she smiled weakly. "No," she pleaded. "Thank you, but no. Please, go to your own family. They will need you this night. You have shown me and my child enough kindness."

"But I ..."

"Please, go. All will be well."

Her words belied her tender years, and Tom felt strangely comforted by them. So he stood up, and glancing back only once, he trudged through the snow not knowing what he was going to find when he got in through the door. His mind flipped between images of his family that he had left that morning and the young woman and her baby he had left in the snow.

An hour later he saw his house, and from the window there was a warm glow as if the fire was blazing. When he went in through the door he was met with the smell of freshly baked bread. There was a ham on the table and potatoes and milk and eggs and butter – more food than he had seen in a very long time.

His wife was smiling. His children looked rosy-cheeked and content. They all clamoured to explain that a strange young woman had called earlier with all this food. All she had said was, "Fear not, all will be well. Your good and kind husband will be home soon."

"What did she look like?" said Tom, and when his wife described her dark eyes and blue homespun shawl, he realized that this Good Samaritan was the same young woman to whom he had given his coat.

Tom told his wife it was nothing short of a blessed miracle. He got down on his knees and gave thanks for it. To his dying day, Tom the blacksmith was a pious man, for he fervently believed that once on a Christmas Eve long, long ago, he had been in the presence of Mary the Virgin Mother and her baby, Jesus.

A Christmas Wish

It's Christmas Eve I'm coming home,
The candle's burning bright.
A welcome in the window
On a perfect winter's night.
Frost is out, no breath of wind,
Big moon shining down.
Ah, but you're not here
On this holy ground.

It's Christmas Day and everyone
Has come in from the cold.
The food is on the table,
We give thanks for gifts untold.
The children are so excited,
The wine is going down,
And I wish you were here
On this holy ground.

It's Christmas night, glass in hand
I'll drink one to your health,
Another to absent friends
And one more for myself,
And when I'm drunk I'll sing this song
Before I lay me down,
For you're not here

On this holy ground.

I know I should be grateful
That you are safe and well,
But I am only human
And I'm missing you like hell.
If I could make a Christmas wish
That would turn this world around,
I'd still wish you here
On this holy ground.

The Miracle of Christmas 1918

It was Christmas in the year 1918. The Great War had only ended six weeks earlier and times were much, much harder than they are nowadays. In a cottage on the side of a hill in the Glens of Antrim lived a woman with her two wee twin daughters, Mary and Agnes. The woman's name was Kathleen O'Connor, and her husband John never came back from Flanders.

Every week for three years she had received a letter from him and a few shillings for housekeep, but for the last six months she'd had no word and not a penny to keep hearth and home together. If that was not bad enough, at the back end of summer she lost her baby son, wee Johnny, as he was called after his father. Kathleen was so worn out with grief and worry, she took bad with her nerves and now she couldn't even lift her head off the pillow.

On Christmas Eve, Mary and Agnes were still hopeful and looking forward to gifts and merriment. A kindly neighbour had been keeping house for the family. In her goodness she had sneaked in a few toffees and such to put in their stockings hanging at the end of the bed. But good cheer would be scarce in the O'Connor house that year.

Early on Christmas morning the twins got themselves ready and set out for first Mass. When the service was over, they waited till everyone had left the chapel so that they could take a closer look at the baby Jesus in the crib. At last, they stole over to the manger and gazed in silence at the wooden doll. It seemed so lifelike. On a whim, Agnes reached in and lifted Jesus out of the manger. She cradled him just the way she had done with her little brother when he was alive.

"Let me have a nurse, Agnes. Please, let me have a go," said Mary.

Then Agnes had an idea. "Let's take the baby Jesus home for Mammy, just for the day. Maybe we could get her to sing again."

"Aye, and we could dress him up in wee Johnny's clothes," said Mary.

Just then they heard a door creaking open and the echo of footsteps. They ran and hid behind the confessional box. Father O'Brien would be so cross if he found the baby Jesus missing from the crib. In their fear they could not help sobbing and sniffling. Then they saw the folds of Father O'Brien's black cassock in front of them, and looked up.

"Come out, Agnes. Come out, Mary," he said, but his voice wasn't angry. "There is someone here who has been looking everywhere for you two."

Well Agnes and Mary crept out from their hiding place. Agnes gave the baby Jesus back to Father O'Brien. When he stepped aside, they saw a man standing in the aisle. He was wearing a long great coat and a peaked cap. Though he was much thinner than in the photograph their mother kept by her bed, they recognized their own father. They ran to him, and he swept them up in his arms and kissed and hugged them, and even the old priest had a tear in his eye.

Hand in hand with their father, Agnes and Mary skipped and chattered the whole way home. Their mother was sitting in the chair by the fire, and for the first time in months there was a smile on her face. The scullery was warm and cosy. There was a jar of mincemeat and a pie and two bottles of mineral water on the table. And there was a doll for each of the twins with beautiful painted faces and real hair. For one day at least they were going to be very, very happy.

Well, the O'Conner family had many trials and tribulations after that – sure haven't we all – but from that year on they always made sure to keep Christmas well. They might have been happier some years, or had more to eat, or received better gifts in the Christmases that followed, but that Christmas of 1918 was the one that lived longest in their memories and burned brightest and in their hearts.

Old Comrades

Well, gentlemen, another year gone by,
As on we march to what ahead may lie.
But we can face the future with heads high
And live with pride until the day we die.

For we were of the fortunate and few,
Young men together once, and then we knew
A brotherhood and loyalty that grew,
As standing side by side our strength we drew.

We can count ourselves blessed among all men,
And harking down the long years back to when
We thought the sword mightier than the pen,
Smile as we remember good times once again.

And if on some dark days we count the cost,
Or shed a tear for friends we may have lost,
Recall the time we cheered and hats were tossed,
And thank the gods that be our paths were crossed.

www.ingramcontent.com/pod-product-compliance
Lightning Source LLC
Chambersburg PA
CBHW040225170726
48295CB00014B/808